CITY OF THE DEAD

A grave matter . . .

"Oh, I almost forgot," Kairn said with a grin. "You'll need this."

He handed Zak a small dagger.

"What for?"

"You have to stick it in the ground in the middle of a grave near the Crypt of the Ancients. Tomorrow morning we'll go and see if it's there. For proof."

So much for his plan. Zak shivered.

"He looks scared!" someone teased.

"Just cold," Zak lied.

"Here, take this." Kairn gave Zak his thick cloak. "And you'll need this, too." He handed Zak a tiny glowrod to use for light.

Zak wrapped the heavy cloak around his shoulders and took a step into the graveyard, holding the glowrod in front of him. Its light barely penetrated the rolling mist. Row after row of tombstones vanished into the darkness before him. He took a few more steps. The headstones looked like a miniature city. A city of the dead.

"Good luck!" Kairn whispered behind him. "Oh, and watch out for the boneworms."

"Boneworms?" Zak hissed. "What are boneworms?"

"Nothing, really," Kairn chuckled. "Just wriggling creatures that come out of the ground. They'll suck the marrow from your bones if you stay still too long!"

The iron gate slammed shut behind Zak.

Look for a preview of Star Wars: Galaxy of Fear #3, *Planet Plague,* in the back of this book!

STAR WARS®
GALAXY of FEAR

BOOK 2

CITY OF THE DEAD

JOHN WHITMAN

BANTAM BOOKS

NEW YORK •TORONTO •LONDON •SYDNEY •AUCKLAND

For my daughter, Sarah, who makes me feel alive

RL 6.0, 008–012

CITY OF THE DEAD

A Bantam Skylark Book / February 1997

ISBN 0-553-48451-6

Published simultaneously in the United States and Canada.

Bantam Books are published by Bantam Books, a division of Bantam Doubleday
Dell Publishing Group, Inc. Its trademark, consisting of the words "Bantam
Books" and the portrayal of a rooster, is Registered in U.S. Patent and Trademark
Office and in other countries. Marca Registrada. Bantam Books, 1540 Broadway,
New York, New York 10036.

PRINTED IN THE UNITED STATES OF AMERICA
OPM   0 9 8 7 6 5 4 3 2 1

PROLOGUE

In his hidden fortress, the scientist strode up to a heavy security door. Next to the door a massive GK-600 guardian droid leveled a heavy blaster cannon and demanded, "Voice recognition and password."

The scientist spoke calmly: "Project Starscream."

"Password verified." The guardian droid lowered its blaster and opened the security door.

The scientist stepped inside his control module. From this command center, he monitored a galactic network of computers and living agents, all working on various aspects of Project Starscream. But only the Emperor, Darth Vader, and he, the scientist, knew Project Starscream's ultimate goal.

"Soon now," the scientist told himself with evil glee, "very soon my power over life and death will be complete. Project Starscream is sure to please the Emperor, and then my control over the galaxy will begin. Nothing can stop me."

An alarm sounded.

The scientist sat down in front of his control module. Above a panel of computer controls sat five viewscreens that allowed the scientist to watch over the five stages of his grand experiment.

One of those viewscreens had just gone blank.

Frowning, the scientist punched a control button. Instantly, streams of information sped across a computer screen. As the scientist read them, his frown deepened.

His first experiment, on the planet D'vouran, had gone off-line. D'vouran was a living planet, a planet he had created as the first part of Project Starscream. Something—*someone*—had caused D'vouran to break free. Now the living planet was spinning through the galaxy, out of control.

Hidden transmitters on the planet had captured images of the intruders just before D'vouran went wild. The scientist saw the images of two human children, a droid, and . . .

. . . *him.*

The scientist let out a snarl of hatred. It couldn't be a coincidence that *he* had been on D'vouran, could it?

For a moment, anger filled the scientist. He reached for a button on his control console. With one command the scientist could order the destruction of Hoole and his companions.

But he did not. His enemy was well known in the galaxy. His murder might attract unwanted attention. And if the Rebels got wind of these experiments, they might try to stop them just as they had stopped the Death Star six months ago.

Instead he pushed a different button. Another one of the viewscreens lit up, and the scientist leaned back into the shadows so that his face could not be seen. On the screen the image of a horribly scarred man appeared.

"Evazan," the scientist demanded, "give me a progress report."

The man on the screen, Evazan, sneered. "I'll give it to you. But first it's time we dispensed with the mystery. I'm tired of working for a faceless man."

From the shadows, the scientist warned, "You are told what you need to know. And you are paid well."

"Not that well," the man called Evazan replied. "You keep hinting that you're someone powerful in the Emperor's inner circle. But for all I know, you're a madman leading me on a wild mynock hunt." Evazan glared at the screen. "Now either you tell me who you are or I take my experiments to the highest bidder."

"That would not be wise."

"Who says?"

"I say." The scientist leaned forward, out of the shadows, at last revealing his face to his hired henchman.

Evazan's eyes widened in surprise. "You!"

"That's correct," the scientist said. "Now listen carefully, or I'll feed you to my Cyborrean battle dogs. You must finish your experiments immediately. I have reason to believe that an old enemy of mine has discovered my work and that he will follow the trail to you."

Evazan sneered. "If any intruders show up here, I'll take care of them."

"Do it quietly," the scientist warned. "And quickly. The being who may try to interfere is more powerful than you suspect. You must destroy him without arousing suspicion."

Evazan nodded. "I have just the means. There's an old superstition on this planet that will provide a perfect cover. Just tell me who the target is."

"His name," the scientist said, "is Hoole."

CHAPTER

Tap. Tap. Tap.

Zak sat up in bed. *What was that noise?*

Something was wrong. He was in his own room, in his own house on the planet Alderaan. But that was impossible.

I can't be here. Alderaan was destroyed by the Empire.

Zak and his sister, Tash, had lost their family, their friends, and their home. They had spent the last six months in the care of their only living relative, an uncle named Hoole.

So Zak knew he couldn't be home, but everything around him looked and felt so real.

Maybe it was all a bad dream! Maybe Alderaan wasn't destroyed. Maybe Mom and Dad are still alive!

To Zak a bad dream would explain a lot. It would explain how his mother and father, and his entire world, could have vanished in a blast of Imperial laser fire. It would explain how he and his sister had been put into the care of their mysterious Uncle Hoole, a shape-changing alien scientist. And it would explain how they had barely escaped from a monstrous planet that had almost eaten them alive.

"It explains things," Zak said out loud, "because that was all a dream. It never happened. And that means I'm home!"

He jumped out of bed.

Tap. Tap. Tap.

That noise had awakened him. Now it repeated itself.

Tap. Tap. Tap.

The noise was coming from outside his bedroom window. Zak got out of bed. His feet felt heavy, and his vision was blurred. He fumbled his way to the transparisteel window. He was about to press the Open button but suddenly stopped.

On the other side of the window, he saw the empty void of deep space.

Deep space? How could his *bedroom* be traveling through deep space?

But it was. In the darkness, Zak could see stars and distant solar systems blazing like tiny points of light.

He rubbed his sleep-filled eyes, but the vision didn't change.

Tap. Tap. Tap.

The sound came from just below his window. Zak resisted the urge to open it. If he did, the vacuum of space would suck him out. He pressed his face against the pane, trying to see what was down there.

Tap. Tap. Tap.

The object started to drift upward into Zak's range of vision. Zak gasped and stumbled back from the window.

A dead, gray hand rose into view.

It was followed by a pale white arm, and then strands of blackened hair. Finally the figure's face floated into view. It was white with empty sockets for eyes, but he recognized the face anyway.

It was his mother.

As he watched in horror, the mouth moved, and Zak heard his mother's voice moan, "Zak, why did you leave us behind?"

Zak screamed.

He opened his eyes.

And found himself sitting up in a bunk onboard the ship known as the *Millennium Falcon*. His bedroom on Alderaan was gone. The corpse was gone. Tash was sitting bolt upright in a nearby bunk.

"Zak! What's the matter?" his older sister cried.

Zak tried to catch his breath. "I—I guess I was dreaming," he finally said. "I dreamed I was in my room . . . but my room was floating in space. And then I saw Mom, but she was floating through space, too. Dead." He squinted to hold back a tear. He couldn't say any more.

Tash walked over to her brother and put a comforting arm around his shoulder. Before she could speak, the door to their small cabin slid open and the snarling face of Chewbacca the Wookiee appeared. He was holding a wicked-looking bowcaster, and his enormous frame filled most of the doorway. Behind him, Tash and Zak could just see the silver frame of the humanoid droid, D-V9.

Chewbacca growled a question.

"I think the Wookiee wants to know what's going on," D-V9 said. "So do I."

D-V9—or Deevee for short—cocked his mechanical head sideways in impatience. The droid had been Uncle Hoole's research assistant for years, until Zak and Tash came along and Hoole had made Deevee their caretaker. Deevee didn't always appreciate his new role, especially when one of his charges caused chaos in the middle of the night.

"It's nothing, Deevee," Zak said. "I just had a bad dream."

"Hey, what's all the shouting?" demanded Han Solo, squeezing past his Wookiee companion.

"Nothing." Tash answered for her brother. "Sorry if we woke you."

"No problem," the starpilot said. "The navicomputer says we're coming up on our destination anyway. Your uncle is in the lounge with Luke and Leia. You might as well get up."

It didn't take Zak and Tash long to get ready. They had lost everything when they were orphaned six months ago. Anything that they had acquired since then, they had lost again only days before, when the planet D'vouran destroyed their ship and nearly took them with it. They had been saved by the *Millennium Falcon* and its crew.

A few moments later, Zak and Tash entered the common area of the *Millennium Falcon,* where Uncle Hoole was waiting for them.

Zak was fascinated by his uncle's appearance. At first glance, Hoole looked like a tall, thin human being—until you noticed that his skin was a light gray color, and his fingers were incredibly long. Hoole, who was only their uncle by marriage, was a member of the Shi'ido species. Although Zak knew that most Shi'ido were quiet and reserved, he could never quite get used to his uncle's grim, brooding personality.

There was another thing about Hoole that Zak couldn't get used to. His uncle was a shape-changer. Like all Shi'ido, Hoole could transform into almost any living creature. Zak had seen it happen more than once. The memory made him shudder.

"Good. You're up," Hoole said. "We will be landing momentarily."

"Landing?" Tash asked.

Hoole nodded. "We need to purchase a new ship. This is the closest inhabited planet."

"What's it called?" Tash asked.

"Necropolis."

"Necropolis?" Zak said. "What a strange name. What does it mean?"

"It means," Hoole said as they felt the *Millennium Falcon* descend into gravity, "City of the Dead."

The *Millennium Falcon* plunged through a swirling mist and landed on a dark platform. With a groan, the ship's hatchway opened, casting pale light onto the ground. The landing pad was built of ancient stone blocks. In the mist-shrouded distance, Tash and Zak could see the shadowy outlines of tall stone buildings crowded together like rows of headstones.

Beside Zak and Tash stood Han Solo, Chewbacca, and the droid companions C-3PO and R2-D2, along with the other friends they had made: Princess Leia, who was from Zak and Tash's home planet, Alderaan, and a young man named Luke Skywalker.

"Boy, you sure can pick them," Han said. "Look at this place."

It was gloomy and depressing. Mist hung heavily in the air, and the darkness gave way reluctantly to light from the *Falcon*'s landing gear.

"Necropolis is a very ancient civilization," Hoole explained. "It has traditions that are thousands of years old."

"Yeah," Zak said, "and it looks like the buildings are even older."

"Look, I hate to say it, but this is as far as we can take you," Han Solo said, patting Zak on the shoulder.

Princess Leia frowned. "Han's right. We've delayed too long already."

"We understand," Tash said. She and Zak suspected that the crew of the *Millennium Falcon* were part of the Rebel Alliance. In fact, Zak had even *asked* them if they were. None of them admitted it, but the way they had acted and the fact that Leia was from Alderaan made Tash and Zak pretty certain that their new friends were Rebels.

"Are you sure you're going to be all right?" Luke Skywalker asked. "We don't want to just abandon you here."

Uncle Hoole answered. "We will be fine. We'll be able to buy a ship here and continue on our way."

Goodbyes were said and thanks were given all around. The droid Artoo-Detoo whistled sadly.

"You're quite right, Artoo," replied his golden counterpart, Threepio. "It is a sentimental moment."

"Touching," Deevee said dryly. "My circuits are overloading with emotion."

Luke said a special goodbye to Tash. She was fascinated by the ancient warriors known as Jedi Knights, and she had taken a liking to Luke since the moment she'd seen his Jedi lightsaber.

He shook her hand respectfully. "Good luck, Tash. May the Force be with you." Then he and his friends returned to their ship.

Zak, Tash, Deevee, and Uncle Hoole watched as the *Falcon*'s hatch closed. Then, with a roar of its powerful engines, the *Falcon* rose into the atmosphere and vanished.

"They were a strange bunch," Zak said. "Nice, but strange. I wonder if we'll ever see them again?"

Tash nodded. "We will."

"How do you know?" her brother asked. But Tash only shrugged. "I just know it."

Zak shook his head. "You're strange, too."

He and Tash followed Uncle Hoole toward one of the dark alleys that led away from the landing pad. The cobblestones beneath their feet were old and slick with moisture. The alley was narrow and lined with what looked like tall, narrow boxes. But as they entered the alley, Zak saw that they weren't boxes. They were very old coffins, open and standing up on their ends.

And they were full.

Inside each coffin Zak saw a human shape draped in a gray burial shroud.

"Ugh!" Zak wrinkled his nose. "Are these . . . mummies?"

"Nonsense," Hoole replied. "Necropolis has an ancient and respected civilization. You must learn to appreciate alien cultures."

Zak didn't hear him. He was too busy staring at the mysterious coffins.

The cloth-wrapped figures stirred. Zak froze in his tracks. One of the mummies had opened its eyes.

CHAPTER

They came out of their cases, staggering toward the small group.

"Welcome to Necropolis," one of the mummies moaned.

Another of the creatures clutched at Tash, and Zak felt a hand grab his shoulder.

"Let go!" he yelled. He tried to push the creature away. To his surprise, the startled mummy stumbled backward and fell to the ground with a grunt.

"Zak!" Uncle Hoole said irritably. "Behave yourself."

"What?" Zak couldn't believe it. His uncle and Deevee looked perfectly calm as the mummies formed a tight circle around them. Then Hoole reached out and shook the hand of the nearest mummy!

Zak was even more surprised when the mummy suddenly removed the shroud from his head. He had the face of a healthy, living human—a very sour-looking human face.

"Uh-oh," Tash whispered.

Zak looked down at the mummy he'd pushed. The rags had slipped off, and beneath them Zak saw a boy his own age, with a big smile on his face.

Deevee shook his chrome-plated head at Zak. "If you spent more time paying attention to my social studies lessons, you might have learned that this is a traditional welcome on Necropolis."

The boy Zak had pushed stood up. "That's right. It's an old tradition. No one really remembers why we do it."

"*I* remember," said the sour-faced man. "Our ancestors did this to scare away the evil spirits that strangers bring. One never knows who might come to wake the dead."

"Wake the dead?" Zak asked. "Are you serious?"

"That's another one of our old Necropolis superstitions. The old-timers believe that if proper respect isn't paid, the dead of Necropolis will rise up." The boy shrugged. "Of course no one believes the old legends anymore except Pylum here."

He pointed to the man, who stiffened. "I am the Master of Cerements, Kairn. It is my duty to make

15

sure the old ways are kept alive so that the ancient Curse of Sycorax does not fall on us."

"What sort of curse?" Zak queried.

Kairn rolled his eyes. "Just a tale-teller's story."

"If you don't believe it, why do you do all this?" Zak asked Kairn.

"Pylum managed to convince our parents that we should learn about the old traditions, so here I am." Kairn shrugged, then flashed a mischievous grin. "Besides, it's fun to scare visitors—except when they get violent!"

Kairn and Zak both laughed.

Once Pylum had finished his traditional welcome and made sure that no "evil spirits" lingered around the visitors, he said they were free to go where they pleased in Necropolis.

"Except the cemetery," the grim man said. "It is sacred ground."

Hoole told Pylum that they had lost their last starship and needed to buy a new one. They also needed a place to stay for the night. Pylum suggested that they try the local hostel.

"Come on, I'll take you there," Kairn offered. "Necropolis is a safe place, but its streets are old and winding, and it's easy to get lost."

The streets of Necropolis were dark, but Kairn's personality was bright enough to light their way. He laughed and chatted as he guided them through the twists and curves of the streets.

He explained the history of Necropolis's culture as they walked. "The legends say that centuries ago, a witch named Sycorax lived in Necropolis. She claimed to have the power to bring back the dead. The people accused her of being a fake, and they did something horrible. They killed the witch's son and told her to bring *him* back to life."

"That's awful," Tash said, shivering.

"Yes, things weren't as peaceful around here in the old days," Kairn said.

"Did it work?" Zak asked. He was very interested in the story. "I mean, was she able to bring her son back from the dead?"

Kairn shook his head. "Instead of bringing her son back, Sycorax died of a broken heart. She and her son were buried together."

"They were what?" Tash asked.

"They were buried."

"Buried?" Zak repeated. "You still bury people?"

Kairn blinked. "Of course. Don't your people do that?"

Deevee, always eager to join a conversation about culture, interrupted. "Oh, quite a few planets inhabited by humans have abandoned that practice," he began cheerily. "They've opted for more efficient methods of body disposal, such as cremation or disintegration. In many cultures, Kairn, burial is considered a bit old-fashioned."

"Not here," Kairn sighed. "My people like the old ways. Necropolitans have been burying their dead for thousands and thousands of years."

Zak almost didn't want to ask his next question. "Where . . . Where do you put them all?" He looked down at his feet, imagining what might be underneath him at that very moment.

There was a mischievous gleam in Kairn's eye. "In the cemetery. Maybe I'll show you."

Deevee returned the discussion to its original topic. "You were telling us about your culture's legend of the witch Sycorax?"

"Right. Just before she died, she cursed the entire planet, saying that if anyone on Necropolis ever ignored the dead, the dead would rise up to take revenge. Ever since then, we Necropolitans have been very careful to keep the dead happy. Believe it or not, the Master of Cerements' only job is to make sure the old rituals are observed. That's what Pylum does."

"You sound like you don't believe it," said Tash.

Kairn snorted. "Those old stories are for little kids. When people die, that's it. They don't come back."

Zak, thinking of his parents, whispered, "I suppose not."

"Here we are!" Kairn announced cheerfully.

They had reached the hostel. Like the rest of Necropolis, the outside of the building was dark and somber. But light streamed through narrow windows on either side of the door, promising warmth inside, and they could hear voices.

"Great!" Zak said. "Let's get out of the gloom."

"Wait, Zak," Tash warned. "Remember what happened last time we strolled into a strange building. We had blasters pointed at our heads."

Hoole studied Tash with sudden seriousness. "Is this one of your feelings, Tash?" the Shi'ido asked.

On D'vouran, Tash had felt a sudden sense of dread come over her. No one had paid attention—not even Tash herself—until it was almost too late. She didn't know how these feelings worked, or what caused them, but obviously Hoole was starting to take them seriously.

"I'm not sure."

"That was then and this is now," Zak said lightly. "It couldn't happen again."

He stepped up to the front door, which opened automatically to reveal a warmly lit room, where a crowd of Necropolitans sat in small groups. Light from a dozen glowpanels shone on delicately carved tables and polished wood floors.

It also gleamed on the barrel of a blaster held in the steady hand of a bounty hunter. It was pointed directly at them.

"My name," the bounty hunter said through an armored helmet, "is Boba Fett."

Tash recognized the name. She'd read about Boba Fett on the intergalactic information service known as the HoloNet. Boba Fett was said to be the greatest bounty hunter in the galaxy. They said he could bring anyone in dead or alive, and he had proved it a hundred times. He had tracked down wanted criminals from one end of the galaxy to the other. Once he accepted a job, no one could escape him.

Boba Fett was covered head to toe in armor and weapons. His face was hidden behind a gleaming metal helmet. His belt and pack bristled with weaponry that included a blaster rifle, deadly wrist rockets, and a nearly unbreakable capture cable. But the most terrifying thing about him was his low, menacing voice, which made Zak think of sliding gravel. Boba Fett spoke to the crowd.

"Where is Dr. Evazan?"

No one spoke. No one moved. Boba Fett was known throughout the galaxy as a deadly shot, and no one wanted his blaster pointed their way.

"What do we do?" Zak whispered.

"Nothing," Uncle Hoole said calmly. But Zak could see that Hoole was intrigued by the bounty hunter's presence. "This is not our concern."

Boba Fett spoke so low that his voice was almost a whisper. "I will say it once more. I tracked a wanted criminal named N'haz Mit to this planet and killed him. A week later I heard N'haz was walking the streets of Necropolis. I had to come back and kill him again. I find that strange."

"Maybe he just got the wrong guy the first time," Tash whispered to Zak.

"Maybe," Zak replied, "but do *you* want to tell him that?"

Boba Fett continued. "My information suggests that Dr. Evazan—the man they call Dr. Death—is somehow responsible."

Fett held up a small holodisk. When he pressed the button, a nearly life-size image appeared next to him.

Dr. Evazan was frightening to behold. Half his face was scarred and mangled, and the other half was turned up in an arrogant sneer. As the hologram hummed, a recorded voice recited: "Name: Evazan. Also known as Dr. Death. Wanted for murder, medical malpractice, practicing medicine without a license, torture, and assault. Posing as a medical doctor, Evazan uses patients as subjects for unauthorized and often fatal experiments. Currently has the death sentence on twelve systems, including—"

"Enough." Boba Fett switched off the holodisk, and the gruesome image of Dr. Evazan vanished. "I want him. Now."

Boba Fett waited.

At first no one spoke. Finally it was Pylum who

answered. "You are mistaken, bounty hunter," he said in a defiant voice. "No scientist is responsible for this mystery. If you saw a dead man walking, it is not because this Dr. Evazan is on our planet. It is because the people have forgotten the old customs. They have abandoned our traditions. They no longer honor those who have passed away." Pylum glared at the crowd. "And because of that, the dead are rising!"

CHAPTER 3

"Ridiculous."

That was all Boba Fett said in response to Pylum's declaration.

The other Necropolitans didn't seem to believe Pylum either. A few of them even hooted and jeered at the Master of Cerements, despite the presence of the bounty hunter. But Pylum continued.

"You'll see," he said, sweeping his fiery gaze across the crowd in the hostel. "The dead are angry, and they will have their revenge."

The armored bounty hunter waited, but no one volunteered any information about Dr. Evazan. Hidden behind his helmet, it was impossible to tell if he was angry, frustrated, or unconcerned. When no one answered his demand, he turned and stalked out of the hostel.

"So that was Boba Fett," Zak breathed. "Prime."

Hoole excused himself to begin his search for their new ship.

"I will return shortly," he said. "Do not leave the hostel grounds." Then, mysterious as always, the Shi'ido slipped out the door.

Zak and Tash spent the rest of the evening at the hostel with their new friend, Kairn. He and Zak took to each other immediately—they had the same sense of mischief and humor. Kairn, it turned out, liked to skimboard as much as Zak did, and they took turns on the hoverboard that Zak kept with him.

Kairn even joined them for dinner at the hostel. When the food was served, the young Necropolitan scooped some of his dinner into a small bowl and put it off to the side without eating it.

"Saving some for later?" Zak joked. He had wolfed down his own food and was about to ask for seconds.

Kairn laughed. "No. It's another old custom. We set aside a portion of every meal in honor of the dead. For most of us, it's more of a tradition now than anything we really believe."

While they ate, Kairn told them more stories about Necropolis and its dark past.

"Lots of legends have built up around the Curse of

Sycorax over the centuries. Pylum says that if you visit the graveyard at midnight, you can ask the witch to bring your loved ones back." Kairn chuckled. "Everyone laughs at those stories in the daytime, but I know a few people who more than half believe it, and some who've even tried it."

"Does it only work on buried people?" Zak asked. Tash, beside him, raised an eyebrow, but Zak ignored her and went on. "I mean, does the legend only work on bodies, or could it work on someone who was . . . disintegrated?"

"I don't know. But Pylum says the power of the curse knows no boundaries."

Pylum suddenly loomed over them. His eyes were filled with eager light. "Our ancestors were fools not to believe in the power of Sycorax. We must believe in the curse of the dead if we are to avoid their mistakes." Pylum glared at them for so long that Zak started to become uncomfortable. Then, without a word, the Master of Cerements turned away.

Tash whispered, "He certainly believes what he's saying, doesn't he?"

Kairn smiled nervously. "He's a fanatic. That's why they made him Master of Cerements."

After dinner Kairn said he had to get home, but he gave Zak a quick wink and whispered, "My friends and I have something fun planned for later. I'll see if I can include you."

Zak grinned. He was always ready for fun and adventure.

"So what do you think?" Zak asked Tash after Kairn had gone.

"Think about what?" she replied.

"About these Necropolitans and their beliefs. You know, that the dead come back."

Tash put down her datapad. "Are you kidding? Zak, that's just a legend. Even the Necropolitans don't believe it. Don't tell me you do."

Zak looked down at his shoes. "Um, of course not. But wouldn't it be prime if people really did come back? I mean, if you could see the people again who—"

"Zak." Tash made her voice as gentle as she could manage. When their parents died, she'd been devastated and hid herself away in her room. But Zak had pulled her out of her misery. Now she wondered if *he* was finally feeling their loss as much as she had. "Zak, I miss Mom and Dad as much as you do. But you can't think that just because of an old superstition, they might actually come back. I know it's hard to think about, but they're gone."

"How do we know?" Zak retorted. Tash could be frustrating. "We weren't there. I didn't tell you my whole dream last night," he confessed. "When I saw—When I saw mom, she also asked me something.

She asked, 'Why did you leave us behind?' Tash, it was like we abandoned them!"

"Stop it, Zak! We didn't abandon them. They were killed by the Empire. The whole planet was. And as much we hate it, we have to accept that Mom and Dad are gone. They're not coming back."

But they did come back. That night. As soon as Zak drifted off to sleep.

Zak again found himself in his bed in his room on Alderaan. He turned his head, and looking out the window, he saw the darkness of space, dotted with stars.

Tap. Tap. Tap.

He heard the sound of someone rapping at the transparisteel window.

Zak tried to sit up but couldn't. A great weight pressed down on his chest, pinning him in place.

Tap. Tap. Tap.

A pale figure floated into the window's view. It was his mother again. Behind her another figure floated: his father, his short hair bobbing in the vacuum of space. Their dead skin hung from their lifeless bones, but their mouths moved in a slow, haunting drawl.

"Zak, why did you leave us behind?"

"I didn't," he said hoarsely, "I thought you were dead!"

"You left us behind!"

Tap! Tap!

Their arms banged against the windowpane until it shattered inward with a crash.

The two ghostly images floated through the opening. Zak struggled to rise, but he was paralyzed. As they approached, Zak's nostrils filled with the smell of slowly decaying flesh. The corpses' skin was wrinkled and cracked from exposure to the icy cold of space. Their eyes were no more than black holes in their skulls.

"Mom," he whispered. "Dad. I'm sorry . . ."

"Come with us, Zak," his father moaned. "Zak, come with us." The horrible image of his father bent close to him, whispering, "Come with us!"

Zak woke with a start. The image of his dead parents vanished. "It was a dream," he said quickly to himself. His window wasn't broken. There was nothing there. "It was only a dream."

Crash! Zak almost screamed as something banged against his window again.

CHAPTER

Zak waited. There were no more crashes.

He finally took a deep breath, and trying to be brave, went over to the transparisteel window and peeked out. There were no monsters or zombies outside. Instead, Zak saw Kairn and a group of boys getting ready to hurl some more stones at his window.

Finally letting his breath out, Zak pressed a button and the automatic window unsealed, letting in the cool night air. He leaned out.

Kairn waved and laughed when he saw Zak. "Sorry about that. I figured you'd want to come with us."

"Where?" Zak asked.

"Some friends and I are having a little midnight adventure. Into the graveyard," Kairn said. "Care to join us? Unless, of course, you're too *scared*?"

Zak couldn't resist a taunt like that. "Wait there. I'm right behind you."

Throwing on some clothes, Zak tiptoed out of his room. He went quietly past the rooms of Tash and Uncle Hoole. At the end of the hall, he froze. There was Deevee, sitting in a chair at the top of the stairs.

"The bionic baby-sitter," Zak muttered. "Looks like this will be one short trip."

But as he crept closer, Zak realized that Deevee had shut himself down for the night. He would not power up unless someone came in range of his sensor field, activating his systems. The field only reached a half meter out from the droid's metal body, but Zak still had no desire to get caught by the sarcastic droid while trying to sneak out.

Better not risk it, he thought. There was always the window.

Zak's room was two levels up from the ground, but the building was covered in elaborate, ghoulish carvings. He started down, using the heads, arms, and claws of the carved monsters as a weird ladder. He stuck his hand into the roaring jaw of a six-legged beast and quietly called down to Kairn, "What are these carvings?"

"Just more legends," Kairn said, holding out his arms, ready to catch Zak. "The statues are supposed to frighten away evil spirits. If you ask me, they make better handholds."

On the ground, Kairn introduced Zak to a small group of Necropolitans, all about his age.

"So this is the offworlder that shoved you, huh?" one of them said to Kairn. "He doesn't look so brave to me."

"Yeah," teased another. "I bet he's an easy scare."

Zak was annoyed. "Are you joking? After the last planet I was on, this place is like a vacation."

"That's just what we wanted to hear!" said Kairn. He lowered his voice to a conspiratorial whisper. "But before you can join our group, there's a little test you have to pass."

"Yeah, we're particular about who joins our group," said another.

"Most people in Necropolis say they don't believe the old legends, but they're still scared of their own shadows," Kairn continued. "At the landing pad you proved you were a little brave, but we need to make sure."

Zak scowled. "What kind of test?"

"Come on, we'll show you."

Kairn led the group of Necropolitan boys down the winding streets of the dark city. Zak followed eagerly. He was on a new planet, walking through a gloomy, alien city in the middle of the night with a group of boys he had only just met, but he felt at home for the first time in months.

Zak had lost all his friends when Alderaan was destroyed. Uncle Hoole hardly talked to him. Deevee was all right, but he wasn't the kind of friend who would help you climb out of your bedroom window in the middle of the night. Tash, Zak had to admit, could be a good friend sometimes, but she was his *sister*—so, in his book, she didn't really count.

But these boys, especially Kairn, reminded Zak of his own group back on Alderaan. They had never caused any real trouble, of course, but they had their share of fun. Once, Zak and some of his friends had snuck into the teachers' washroom at their school and replaced the mirror with a hologram screen programmed to reflect anyone's image exactly—only twenty kilos heavier. Snack sales at the instructors' cantina had plummeted until the prank was discovered.

Now, for the first time in half a year, Zak felt like he had a chance to have some real fun. He decided instantly that he was going to make the most of it. By the time they reached their destination, Zak was laughing and joking with Kairn like they were old friends.

"This is it," Kairn said as they stopped in front of a huge, black wrought-iron gate.

Zak couldn't see beyond the thick mist of Necropolis. "What is it?"

One of the other boys said ominously, "It's the cemetery."

"The boneyard," Kairn added.

"Sacred ground!" said another in his best imitation of Pylum. They all laughed.

But Zak was too awestruck to smile. The cemetery was enormous. Beyond the black gates, row upon row of gravestones stretched on forever into the darkness.

"It's huge," he whispered.

"That's the true Necropolis," Kairn said. "The city of the dead."

"It's the most popular place in town," one of the others joked. "Everyone goes there. Eventually."

Zak asked, "You mean everyone's buried here? It must be crowded."

"I suppose, but so far no one's complained," Kairn said, laughing. "Here's the challenge. You have to go into the graveyard in the dead of night and stand on a grave in the middle of the cemetery."

"Go in there?" Zak asked hoarsely. He peered through the gate, imagining the rows of dead stacked just below the ground.

"Sure," Kairn said. "What have you got to lose?"

"His nerve," one of the others teased.

Zak considered. "If I accepted, what else would I have to do?"

Kairn grinned. "Not much. Just get to the middle of the cemetery and back."

Zak peered through the iron gates. The mist made it hard to see. Through the drifting clouds of gray fog, he could just barely make out the first line of headstones in the darkness.

"Maybe he's too scared after all," said one of the boys.

"I'm not scared," Zak insisted.

The mist is so thick, he thought, *that they'll hardly be able to see me ten meters beyond the gate. How will they know how far I've gone?*

"It's a bet," he said with a gleam in his eye.

"Good." Kairn said. "All you have to do is go in and follow any path. They all lead to the center of the graveyard, where you'll see a large tomb. That's the Crypt of the Ancients. According to legend, that's where they buried Sycorax and her son. Pick any of the graves around the crypt, stand right on top of it, and then come back."

The wrought-iron gate was locked. Zak watched in amazement as one of Kairn's smallest friends managed to squeeze through the bars of the gate. He went to a control panel on the inside wall and pressed some buttons. The gates swung open with a mournful squeal. Zak was about to step in when his new friend stopped him.

"Oh, I almost forgot," Kairn said with a grin. "You'll need this."

He handed Zak a small dagger.

"What for?"

"You have to stick it in the ground in the middle of a grave near the Crypt of the Ancients. Tomorrow morning we'll go and see if it's there. For proof."

So much for his plan. Zak shivered.

"He looks scared!" someone teased.

"Just cold," Zak lied.

"Here, take this." Kairn gave Zak his thick cloak. "And you'll need this, too." He handed Zak a tiny glowrod to use for light.

Zak wrapped the heavy cloak around his shoulders and took a step into the graveyard, holding the glowrod in front of him. Its light barely penetrated the rolling mist. Row after row of tombstones vanished into the darkness before him. He took a few more steps. The headstones looked like a miniature city. A city of the dead.

"Good luck!" Kairn whispered behind him. "Oh, and watch out for the boneworms."

"Boneworms?" Zak hissed. "What are boneworms?"

"Nothing, really," Kairn chuckled. "Just wriggling creatures that come out of the ground. They'll suck the marrow from your bones if you stay still too long!"

The iron gate slammed shut behind Zak.

CHAPTER

Zak looked around. He stood at the edge of the grave-yard, which stretched out before him into the misty dark. Winding among the headstones, Zak saw several flagstone paths.

"The paths of the dead," Zak said to himself.

He stopped to look at the nearest grave marker. There were words carved on it in a language he couldn't read, but Zak could guess what it said. He whispered, "Here lies someone's loving mother, laid to rest by her adoring family."

Zak bit his lip. His parents had never been laid to rest.

Maybe that's why they were haunting him. Maybe that's why his parents had visited him twice in his dreams. He was sure they would visit him again.

Were they angry at him because he wasn't with

them when they died? Because he and Tash hadn't given them a proper burial? That's what the Necropolitans believed.

But how could we? he thought. *The whole planet was destroyed.*

Zak's brain knew that, but his heart didn't. His heart was full of guilt because he had not been able to give his parents a funeral. He hadn't had a chance to say goodbye.

The Necropolitans are right, he thought. *If you don't give the dead their respect, they* do *come back to haunt you.*

A muffled crunching noise made Zak jump. He looked around but saw nothing in the dark. He shivered, and stopped to pull the heavy cloak tight around his shoulders. He had to get this over with and stop thinking about such creepy things.

Zak wasn't a thinker like Tash was. She read everything she could get her hands on, especially about the mysterious Jedi Knights. She talked about philosophy and even believed in a mystical power called the Force. Zak preferred to think with his hands, and was a born tinkerer. He would take apart a repulsor lift just to see if he could put it together again. When he wasn't building things, he was pulling daredevil stunts in the hologym or on his skimboard.

Maybe the stunts are getting a little out of hand, he thought, looking around the deserted cemetery.

The crunching sound came from directly beneath his feet.

Zak jumped almost a meter into the air. He looked down just in time to see a gleaming slimy white shape wriggle into the ground right where he had been standing.

Boneworms.

He remembered Kairn's warning and decided not to stand in one place for too long.

As he continued along the path, Zak admitted to himself what he had hinted to Tash. He had been skeptical of Tash and her all-powerful "Force," but he wanted to believe in the powers of the witch of Necropolis, and he hoped the Necropolitans were right. Then maybe his mother and father could come back. And then he'd be able to see them and say goodbye.

That was the real reason Zak had come to the graveyard.

Despite the cobblestone path, Zak soon found himself lost in a maze of tombs and graves. The cemetery seemed to go on forever. Now and then Zak thought of turning back, but he didn't want to face the teasing his new friends would give him, and he knew that he wouldn't be able to rest until he had at least tried the thing he was planning.

He walked for what seemed like an hour. But with all the twists and turns, he doubted that he was more than half a kilometer from the iron gates. Just as he was about to give up, he turned yet another corner and found himself before an enormous crypt. Its face was carved with rows of horned creatures that looked like krayt dragons, their leering faces warning him to stay away. A massive iron door was set in the wall of the crypt. Oddly enough, there was a strong lock on the outside of the door, as though the Necropolitans were trying to keep someone—or some*thing*—inside.

"This has got to be the place," Zak said to the darkness. "The Crypt of the Ancients."

He stood before the iron door and took a deep breath. "Um, excuse me," he said out loud. He felt foolish, but so what? He'd do anything to bring his parents back. "My name is Zak Arranda. I'm not from Necropolis. I don't know if that matters. But my parents are gone. And I didn't get a chance to say good-bye." As he spoke, the feeling of foolishness was replaced by something else. Hot tears welled up in his eyes. "It's not fair that they were taken away from us! Especially not like that. We didn't even get a chance to see them! And now I miss them so much. I'd give anything to be able to see them again, just once. Not the way I see them in my nightmares, I mean really *see* them and talk to them. That's why I came here. If you really were a witch, if you really did have the power to bring back the dead, this is for a good cause. So won't you help me? Please?"

He waited.

Nothing happened.

The iron door remained as solid and cold as the moment before he spoke.

"Stupid idea. . . ." Zak felt foolish once again. He sniffed back his last tear. "Thinking that something like this would work. Next thing you know you'll be muttering about the Force and wishing you were a Jedi like Tash."

Zak remembered the bet with his friends. He looked around and saw that there were several smaller graves around the Crypt of the Ancients. He walked over to one and pulled out the small knife Kairn had given him. He hesitated for a moment when he realized that he would have to stand on the grave to stick the knife into the ground. What would it be like to stand on a grave? Zak took one careful step onto the burial plot. Was it his imagination or did the ground seem softer, squishier?

"It's your imagination," he told himself.

Still, how would he feel if someone stood on his grave?

"I wouldn't feel anything," he told himself.

Zak took another step. Now he was standing right on the grave. He couldn't help but imagine that his weight was pushing down on the ground, which was pushing down on a coffin, squeezing a lifeless body less than two meters beneath his feet. He waited, his heart pounding.

Nothing happened.

Of course nothing happened, he thought. *You're being ridiculous.*

Shrugging off his fear, Zak raised the knife high into the air, hesitated just a moment, and then plunged the knife into the ground.

For a moment Zak froze again. He heard a muffled sound below him. He turned quickly, ready to run.

Just as he did, a long, low moan rose up from the beneath his feet. The ground shuddered.

And a hand reached up through the dirt.

CHAPTER

6

The moment he saw the gnarled white hand, Zak yelled in terror and started to run.

He took only a few steps before he saw the ground in front of him also tremble. Clods of soil shot up as wriggling arms forced their way to the surface, followed by the ghastly, grinning faces of two zombies. They twitched violently, but with every spasm they crawled farther out of the holes into which they'd been placed. Like Zak's nightmare vision of his parents, the creatures' pale skin hung limply from their bones. A few thin strands of dead gray hair clung to the sides of their heads. Inside one of the monsters' slack jaw, Zak could see a thick tongue lying like a dead worm.

Zak was so frightened by the two undead creatures

before him that he'd forgotten about the first one. When he tried to run, he felt something incredibly strong grab the hem of his cloak, holding him back.

"Let go of me!" he shouted, wriggling free of the cloak. He let it fall to the ground behind him as he ran for his life.

Zak ran so fast that soon he had left the zombies behind, swallowed up in the great fog bank that hung over the cemetery. He had lost them.

Unfortunately he had lost himself, too.

Zak was no longer on the path he had taken to the Crypt of the Ancients. He didn't know which way to turn. All he could see were rows of headstones. There were thousands of them! Even worse, Zak had no idea when another dead body might spring out of its grave to grab him.

Zak's heart was racing. He couldn't believe what he had just seen. It was impossible, but it had happened. The dead had risen. Three people had dug themselves out of their own graves!

Could I have caused it? he wondered. *Have I offended the dead?*

Whether he had caused it or not, Zak wanted out of the cemetery.

"Help!" he shouted. "Someone help!"

A distant voice returned his cry. Zak ran toward the

sound of the crying voice. "Who's there?" he called out. "Where are you?"

He heard the voice cry out again and thought he recognized it as Kairn's. Kairn had come to help him! Zak hurried toward the sound, keeping an eye out for any more of the terrifying creatures. They didn't seem to move very quickly, but he didn't want to end up in that cold, powerful grip again.

"Kairn! Kairn, is that you?"

"Zak! Where are you?" Kairn's voice came from out of the mist.

"Here! Here!" he called. "Where are *you*?"

"I'm over—*aaagh!*" Kairn's shout was cut off with a strangled cry.

"Kairn!" Zak ran even faster, forgetting where he was and vaulting over headstones as he raced to where he thought his friend must be.

A figure materialized out of the fog. For a fraction of a second, Zak's heart skipped a beat. Another zombie?

But the figure wasn't moving. It was about Kairn's size and shape, and it slumped against a large rounded headstone.

"Kairn, is that you?" Zak said as he slowed to a halt. The mist was so thick that he could hardly see the figure's face. He peered closer. The eyes were wide with horror. The mouth was open, and something red dripped from one corner.

"Kairn!" Zak yelled.

"He's dead," a hard voice said. "And it looks like you're next."

Zak whirled around. There was the brutally scarred face he recognized from the hologram image Boba Fett had shown them: the face of Dr. Evazan.

Also known as Dr. Death.

CHAPTER

Half of Dr. Evazan's face looked normal enough, but the other half was covered in scars and sores.

"I can't believe my luck," Evazan said, grinning from the undamaged side of his face. "It looks like I'll have two patients to care for this evening. Come on, boy, let the doctor have a look at you."

With lightning speed, one hand shot out and grabbed Zak by the hair.

"Ow!" Zak winced. "What did you do to Kairn?"

"The same thing I'll do to you in just a moment," said Dr. Evazan. Evazan's voice was chillingly calm. "I need subjects to work on if I'm going to continue my experiments. Healthy young subjects like him. And you."

Zak's head was tilted backward so he couldn't move it, forcing his mouth open. In his other hand, Dr. Evazan held some kind of blood-red berry. He crushed the berries in his hand so that the juice dripped out of his palm and into Zak's mouth.

"That's it," Evazan cooed. "Swallow the berry juice and it will all be over."

Zak tried not to swallow. The juice was bitter and made him gag. If he could only free himself!

"Evazan."

The voice that spoke was as cold as deepest space.

The voice of Boba Fett.

Another criminal might have turned to look. Not Dr. Evazan. The moment his name was spoken, the evil doctor released Zak and dove for cover behind a headstone. A blaster bolt shattered the writing on the face of the grave marker.

Free, Zak spat out the vile-tasting juice and wiped his mouth. He ran to where Boba Fett stood as still and calm as a statue.

"Th-thanks!" Zak cried. "He was going to—"

"Silence." Fett didn't even look at Zak. Fett scanned the terrain and then nodded to himself, as though seeing something Zak could not. "Remain here."

"But we've got to get out of here! There are corpses coming out of the ground and . . ."

With one hand, Fett grabbed Zak by the shirt collar and pushed him gently but firmly to the ground until Zak's ear was pressed against the moist dirt.

"Remain here," Fett repeated. Holding his blaster at the ready, the armored killer strode silently off into the darkness.

Lying there without his borrowed cloak, afraid to move, Zak wondered if he was in shock. Kairn's lifeless body lay a few feet away, the dead eyes staring right into Zak.

To make things worse, somewhere nearby, the dead were waking.

Zak felt something brush across his cheek. He wiped his hand across his face and felt something wet and squishy stick to his hand. When he looked, he saw a plump, wriggling white worm wrap itself around his hand. One end of the boneworm pressed itself against Zak's skin, and he felt a sharp pain, as though something were gnawing at him. He gasped and flicked the boneworm away.

He wasn't sure how much more of this he could take. If he moved, he was afraid Boba Fett would shoot him. If he didn't move, one of the zombies might find him, or the boneworms might eat him alive.

Zak felt something else brush across his cheek, but when he reached for it, his hand touched the cold muzzle of a blaster.

Dr. Evazan had found him. "Get up!"

Without waiting for Zak to obey, Evazan hauled him up and pressed the blaster to his back. "You're my little passport out of this mess. Fett's a killer, but they say he's choosy about who he sends into the void. You will do as you're told, understand?"

Zak managed a nod.

Evazan held Zak before him like a shield as he stalked cautiously down the path. After only a moment, they saw Boba Fett's bullet-shaped helmet rise up before them in the gloom.

"Don't fire, Fett!" Dr. Evazan warned. "I have the boy with me. So unless you want innocent blood on your hands, don't make any sudden moves."

The figure of Boba Fett remained frozen.

"Ha!" Evazan sneered as he took a few cautious steps forward. "Perhaps your reputation is greater than your skills, bounty hunter. You let me backtrack you and get to the boy. You should have known that was my only chance. That was your last mistake."

Evazan took a few more steps toward the armored figure.

"Perhaps you're not really as good as they say, eh?"

Another step.

"Perhaps I should destroy you right now. Put you out of your misery."

Evazan was close enough to touch Fett now. Fett

stood before him, absolutely motionless. Still holding tightly onto Zak, Evazan reached forward and jabbed the bounty hunter with his blaster.

The armor, helmet and all, fell apart and clattered to the ground.

"Wh—?" Evazan started to say.

He never finished. A blaster bolt screamed through the air. Noise and light exploded around Zak, and beside him, Evazan screamed once, then slumped forward.

"Don't turn around." It was Boba Fett. Even without the helmet to filter his voice, the bounty hunter sounded cold as durasteel.

Zak realized that Boba Fett was standing behind him, completely unmasked. All he had to do was turn around, and he would see the face that few had ever seen, the face of the galaxy's most relentless hunter.

He didn't turn around.

"Pick up the helmet." Zak obeyed. "Hand it backward over your shoulder."

Zak kept his eyes forward and did as he was told. The helmet was snatched out of his hand. He heard an electronic snap as fittings locked into place. He knew then that he could turn around.

Boba Fett stood before him, wearing only a jumpsuit and his helmet, and holding his blaster.

"You tricked him," Zak said.

Boba Fett said nothing. The bounty hunter retrieved

his armor and pulled a small holorecorder from his pocket. He bent down to examine Dr. Evazan's body.

Zak watched. "Is he—?"

"Dead," Boba Fett said into the recorder. "Termination of Dr. Evazan, also known as Dr. Death, confirmed by holoscan with medical uplink. Payment now due from twelve planetary systems." Fett snapped the recorder off and tucked it back into its pocket. Then, with smooth efficiency, he began to put his armor back on.

Zak stammered, "He—he was going to kill me. You saved my life. Thanks."

The bounty hunter spared the slightest glance. "Thanks are inappropriate. You were incidental."

Suddenly Boba Fett straightened and drew his blaster faster than the eye could follow. He seemed to be listening. Zak listened, too, but at first he heard nothing. Then, finally, the sound of approaching footsteps reached his ears.

"Zak! Zak!"

He heard familiar voices call out through the mist.

"Tash! Uncle Hoole! Over here! We have to help Kairn!" he called back.

It took a few more blind shouts, but finally Tash, Deevee, and Hoole found Zak. They were accompanied by a small band of Necropolitans led by Pylum, the Master of Cerements, who looked furious.

By this time Boba Fett was once again wearing his

armored shell. The bounty hunter stood calmly by as Zak ran to his sister and uncle. "He's dead! Uncle Hoole, Kairn's dead!"

"Zak, what is going on? What are you doing out here?" Hoole demanded.

Zak shivered. His fear was wearing off, and he realized he was very cold. "I came out here on a dare, Uncle Hoole. But that doesn't matter! Kairn's dead! And I saw something—something you're not going to believe. The Necropolitans are right! The dead are coming out of their graves!"

Hoole's brow wrinkled. "What are you babbling about? We heard blaster fire."

"That was him," Zak said, pointing to Boba Fett. "He killed Dr. Evazan."

"Who?" Hoole asked.

"Dr. Evazan. The wanted man he was hunting. Him."

Zak pointed to Evazan's lifeless body.

"I tracked down a bounty," Boba Fett said. "Evazan is dead. Now I will take the body."

"You cannot do that," Pylum protested. "That would be a terrible violation of our laws. The dead—even criminals—must be buried immediately, otherwise the Curse of Sycorax will be on all our heads. We will give this body the proper ceremonies."

Boba Fett stared coldly at Pylum for a moment. Zak had the distinct impression that the bounty hunter was trying to decide whether or not to vaporize Pylum with his blaster.

Apparently Fett decided he wasn't worth the trouble. "Very well. I have recorded the death, and you are all witnesses. If I do not collect my bounty from the proper authorities, I will return to collect it from you."

With those words the armored assassin turned and walked away until he was swallowed up by the darkness.

Meanwhile Pylum had examined Kairn's body, especially the red liquid on the side of his mouth. The Master of Cerements stood up and shook his head. "Cryptberries. They grow around the graveyards, and they are extremely dangerous. The boy has poisoned himself with cryptberries."

"He didn't poison himself," Zak said. "It was Evazan. He tried to do the same thing to me. And before that, I saw corpses crawling out of their graves!"

"I warned you," Pylum said. "The dead are rising! The Curse of Sycorax is real!"

"Ridiculous," Hoole snorted. "Show me these empty graves."

Zak was frightened. He could see that no one believed him. They returned to the Crypt of the Ancients, led by Pylum. Hoole and the others shone glowrods all around the crypt.

But the graves were undisturbed.

CHAPTER

"That's impossible," Zak whispered. "There were creatures. Zombies! Dig up the graves. You'll see that they're empty."

"We cannot do that!" Pylum argued. "That would be the worst crime of all. The dead would never forgive us."

"But you've got to believe me!"

"Calm down, Zak," his uncle insisted. "Tell us exactly what happened."

Zak sighed. "I came into the graveyard on a dare. I was supposed to stick a knife in one of the graves to prove I'd gone all the way to the center of the cemetery. But when I did, the bodies started crawling out of the ground!" Zak could tell that no one believed him. "At first I didn't see anything, but I heard noises coming from underground."

"The ground settling, most likely," Deevee said, tapping the dirt with one metallic foot. "All the soil here is loose from so many burials."

"But then I saw them . . . dead-white shapes moving in the darkness."

"Boneworms," Deevee suggested. "You must have seen boneworms crawling on the topsoil."

Zak was growing frustrated. "Oh? Then what about my cloak? Kairn loaned me his cloak, and one of the zombies tore it right off my shoulders. It should be around here somewhere."

"Here it is," Hoole said. He held a glowrod over the dropped cloak. "And here's your explanation."

The edge of the cloak was pinned to the ground by the knife Zak had stuck into the grave. "You must have caught the edge of the cloak when you stuck the knife in. You only thought someone was grabbing you."

"But I saw them!" Zak insisted.

Pylum cut in on their conversation. The Necropolitan jabbed one finger at Zak while speaking to Hoole. "It does not matter what the boy thinks did or did not happen. The fact is, he intruded on sacred ground. He has broken the ancient laws and must be punished in the ancient ways."

The Shi'ido's frown deepened. "I'm afraid I can't allow that. Zak shouldn't have come in here, but he didn't know anything about your laws, and he didn't mean any harm."

"The strangers are right, Pylum," one of the other Necropolitans said. "We can't punish offworlders for laws they don't know about."

Pylum disagreed. "This boy's mischief led to the death of one of our own."

"Evazan killed him!" Zak said.

"Will you believe this boy?" Pylum asked his companions. "Or the laws of Necropolis?"

"Let them go, Pylum," said another Necropolitan. "This boy's been through enough for one evening."

Outnumbered, Pylum could do nothing. But he threw Zak an angry glare that said, *You haven't heard the last of me.*

Hoole led his niece and nephew away from the cemetery. A solemn crowd followed them, carrying the bodies of Dr. Evazan and Kairn.

Tash Arranda worried all the way home, and stayed worried even after Hoole and Deevee had seen her and her brother to their rooms. Zak hadn't said a word, and he was silent all the way back to his room, where he locked the door behind him.

The next morning, Zak stayed in his room during breakfast. For Zak, who usually ate anything and everything in sight, that was a sure sign something was wrong.

Tash decided to tease him out of his sullen mood and knocked on his door. He opened it with a scowl.

56

"Hey, rancor breath," she said.

"Hey."

"What's this? No comebacks? No insults? You're slowing down on me, blaster brain."

Zak's face darkened. "I'm not in the mood, Tash, so leave me alone."

She tried her best to sound cheery. "Nope. Can't do it. You're my brother, and it's my job to see that you get insulted as often as possible."

Zak slapped a button on the wall, and the door shut in Tash's face.

Wrong approach, Tash decided.

She wondered whether he was simply in shock from the death of his new friend. She could understand if he was upset about Kairn. It was terrible when anyone died, but to have it happen to such a happy, friendly person was even worse. And he was Zak's first real friend in awhile. It made sense. Still, it wasn't like Zak to shut himself away when he was upset, even at something like that.

Maybe he was angry that no one believed his story about the zombies. But how *could* anyone believe him? Who had ever heard of the dead coming back to life? Besides, even if Zak believed his own story, he was too stubborn and independent to let someone else's opinion depress him. He'd just ignore them.

It had to be something else about his adventure in the cemetery. But what?

Deevee came out of Uncle Hoole's room and stopped beside Tash. "Still no luck in exhuming our buried young Zak?"

"Exhume," Tash said, ignoring Deevee's poor taste in jokes. "That means to dig up, right?"

"Ah, I see our lessons are paying off at last," Deevee replied.

"This is no time for jokes, Deevee."

The droid gave his mechanical version of a shrug. "Not to worry. Before you know it, Zak will rise up like the dead of the Necropolitan legends. Now if you'll excuse me, I have to continue Master Hoole's search for a suitable ship."

Tash repeated Deevee's words to herself. "Like the dead of the Necropolitan legends." Like Zak, Tash had heard the stories about people who visited the Crypt of the Ancients, hoping to bring people back from the dead.

Is that what Zak had wanted to do?

"I guess it didn't work, did it?" she called through the door. "Trying to bring Mom and Dad back, I mean."

There was a pause. Then the door opened and Zak let her in. "You didn't go into that cemetery just because someone dared you, did you?" Tash guessed. "You went in because you thought there was some way to bring Mom and Dad back."

Zak reddened. "Yeah. Pretty stupid, huh?"

"I don't know," she said. "If I thought there was some way to get them back, I'd try it, too. But, Zak, even Kairn said that story's just a legend."

It's not a legend, Zak thought. *I saw it happen. The dead can come back!*

However, he knew Tash wouldn't believe him. She and Deevee and Uncle Hoole thought he was imagining things. Out loud, he said, "Maybe you're right, Tash."

Tash grinned. "Hey, I'm always right!"

Tash left Zak's room feeling like she'd helped him—at least a little. He was obviously very bothered. What had started as one scary nightmare had turned into a series of delusions about walking corpses. But she was confident that he would snap out of it.

Tash headed for her room down the hall. As she did, she passed by Uncle Hoole's room. The door was closed, but the sound of conversation leaked through.

Conversation? Hadn't Deevee gone off to look at starships? Who would Uncle Hoole be talking to?

Curious, Tash listened closely, and her eyes grew wide with surprise.

"In any case, that is my proposal," came the voice of Uncle Hoole.

"I'll consider it," replied another voice.

The voice of Boba Fett.

CHAPTER

By midday Tash was kicking herself for not opening Uncle Hoole's door right then and there. But she had been too surprised. Why was a respectable scientist like Uncle Hoole talking to a notorious bounty hunter like Boba Fett?

By the time she had recovered her wits, the voices were approaching the door, and Tash had barely scrambled around a corner before Hoole's door slid open. She caught only a glimpse of the armored assassin striding out of Hoole's quarters.

They had to attend Kairn's funeral that afternoon. "The funeral rites of Necropolis are most impressive," Deevee said on the way to the cemetery. "I wish I could attend! Unfortunately my search for a reliable starship dealer continues. Otherwise I wouldn't miss the funeral. It should be most interesting to watch."

"Deevee!" Tash scolded. "This isn't a field trip. It's a solemn occasion."

That it was.

A great many people turned out for the funeral. Zak and Tash weren't surprised that Kairn had so many friends.

At the cemetery gates, the crowd gathered around an elegantly carved coffin. Necropolitan symbols were carved into its lid, and Zak noticed that although the coffin lid was shut, there was a large bolt on it that had not yet been locked.

Next to the coffin, a small, closed tent had been erected. Zak could not see inside, but he heard someone sobbing.

"Uncle Hoole, what's that tent for?" he asked quietly.

Hoole replied, "Kairn's parents are in there. The Necropolitans believe that if the dead see the living mourn, they might come back. In order to prevent that, the family of the departed live in seclusion for seven days. No one sees them."

A day ago Zak would have shaken his head at such superstitious nonsense. But he now knew the dead could come back. He had seen it.

The muttering of the crowd stopped as Pylum, the

Master of Cerements, stopped before the coffin. The sour-faced Necropolitan stood at the edge of the cemetery and delivered a long speech about the dangers of disturbing the dead.

"The old ways are the true ways," Pylum intoned. "The dead must be respected. The dead must be left undisturbed. The alternative is disaster. That is the way of Necropolis."

As Pylum talked, Zak couldn't help feeling a pang of guilt. His parents had had no funeral. No one had offered them a show of mourning, even in private. No one had done anything for them.

No wonder they haunted his dreams.

Pylum raised his voice, snapping Zak out of his reverie.

"May the spirit of Sycorax receive this departed being in peace. May Kairn, who is gone from the living, remain now forever in the city of the dead!"

With that, Pylum grabbed the heavy bolt attached to the coffin, and with a dramatic flourish, he slammed it into place, sealing the coffin forever.

From behind the curtains of the pavilion, Zak heard a low, sad wail.

The crowd followed as Pylum led the coffin-bearers—some of whom Zak recognized from the night before—into the cemetery. Zak noticed that the Necropolitans were very careful to stay on the paths and to avoid the ground near the graves.

The caravan moved silently until they reached an open grave. It was as if they were frightened to speak too loudly, afraid that even a whisper might disturb the dead. Silently, the coffin-bearers lowered Kairn's coffin into the grave and slowly shoveled dirt over it.

As the mourners walked out of the cemetery, Zak passed by a freshly dug grave. The gravestone was written in the Necropolitan language and in Basic, the common language of the galaxy. It read: "Here lies Dr. Evazan. May he find the peace he did not give his patients."

That, Zak thought, *is putting it lightly.*

They returned to the hostel to find Deevee waiting for them.

"It took great effort, and I think I actually used a fraction of my computer brain to do it, but I've located a dealer in starships who had several vessels for sale," Devee said.

Tash and Zak soon found themselves trailing behind their Shi'ido uncle and his droid assistant as they wound their way through the avenues of Necropolis, on their way to the starship dealer.

Although the sun was out, Necropolis was covered by the same feeling of darkness that had filled it at night. The old stone buildings were so tall and wide that very little sunlight reached the streets, and down among the walkways it seemed like midnight at noon.

Tash watched Uncle Hoole as he walked in front of

her. She had been suspicious of him for some time. He was supposed to be an anthropologist, devoting his scientific mind to the study of different species and cultures across the galaxy. But although they had lived with him for six months, he still had not told them anything about himself—not even his first name. And even though he knew an awful lot about science, he acted like no scientist Tash had ever heard of.

He had no laboratory. He ran no experiments. Whenever they arrived on a new planet, he often went out on midnight errands and refused to tell anyone where he was going.

Not long ago Tash and Zak had had a run-in with the gangster Smada the Hutt. The vile crime lord had somehow known Hoole. Hoole had claimed that he had once refused to work for the Hutt gangster, and Tash had believed him. But at the same time, Smada had hinted that Hoole was involved in some shadowy schemes—that maybe he even had ties to the Empire. And now Hoole was working with Boba Fett, one of the most vicious killers in the galaxy. It was too much of a coincidence.

These thoughts filled Tash's mind. She was so pre-occupied that before she knew it, they had arrived at an immense dockyard at the edge of Necropolis. The enormous yard was a weird mixture of old and new. Ancient stone buildings surrounded it, but the open space was filled with modern, automated maintenance equipment and sleek, modern starships.

"Welcome, welcome, welcome!"

A Necropolitan greeted them with wide-open arms and an even wider grin. He walked right up to Hoole and put his arm around the scientist's shoulder. "Welcome to Meego's Starship Emporium, where we don't bring the stars to you. We bring *you* to the stars! I'm Meego. What can I do for you?"

Uncle Hoole opened his mouth to speak, but Meego continued. "Wait, lemme guess. You're looking for a family star cruiser. Something you and the kids can tool around in. Visit the Hologram Fun World, maybe do some sight-seeing in the Outer Rim. I've got just the thing. Right this way!"

He tried to drag Hoole toward a sleek new star cruiser that looked expensive. Hoole stood as still as a statue. "That particular ship may be out of my price range."

Meego was undaunted. "On a budget? Aren't we all? But I'm sure we can work out some financing. And believe me, this is the kind of ship that'll pay for itself in no time. Besides, with an energetic family like yours you'll—"

"Need the room?" Tash interrupted.

"Exactly," said Meego, still talking to Hoole. "And I can tell from your attitude that you're not just a tourist. You travel for a living, am I right? You'll need—"

"To be comfortable," Tash ended.

"Right again. And don't forget about—"

"Dependability? Low cost of repairs? Style?" Tash guessed. The dealer looked annoyed. Tash had somehow figured out everything he was about to say.

Zak recognized the look on the dealer's face. "Don't mind her," he said. "She does that a lot."

Tash only smiled. Her little gift came easy with this ship dealer—maybe because his thoughts were so shallow.

"How . . . delightful," the dealer sputtered. He seemed irritated that she had interrupted his speech and tried to get back on track. "Well, come on, it won't cost you anything to look . . ."

The dealer's mouth ran faster than a hyperdrive engine. Zak groaned inwardly. He was only thirteen, and he still had a lot to learn about starships. But he knew enough to see that the starship the salesman was pushing was all looks and no power. His eyes wandered over to a ship tucked in an unlit corner of the dockyard.

"Now that," Zak said aloud, "is a ship. What about that one?"

"That looks like a used ship," Tash pointed out.

The salesman winced. "We prefer the term 'preowned.' We just acquired it from its previous owner, who is, um, deceased. I'm afraid it's not yet available for sale."

The fast-talking salesman managed to lure Uncle Hoole over to the new ship, but Zak didn't follow. His feet turned automatically in the direction his eyes were looking. Zak recognized the "pre-owned" ship from star catalogs. It was an Arakyd Helix Interceptor. Even docked, the Interceptor looked like an angry bird of prey. Its forward hold stuck out like a wicked beak, and its hull curved downward like sloping wings. Black streaks ran along its side and bottom where it had been burned making rushed entries into the atmosphere. Its landing gear looked battered from landings and takeoffs that were too fast.

But all that was meaningless. Sleek, durachrome exteriors were just candy for the eyes. Smart pilots looked at one thing: the engine, and the engine on this ship was . . .

"Prime," Zak said to himself. "That's an Incom GBp-629 with a backup hyperdrive motivator and double-reinforced power couplings." Which meant, simply, that the ship could go very, very fast.

Zak walked around the ship, examining the fittings and power cable connections. Most of the fine points were too technical for him, but he had studied enough to know that some of the modifications on that ship were illegal. He had seen that kind of custom fitting on only one other ship: the *Millennium Falcon*.

Which means this ship belonged to a smuggler . . . or a pirate, he decided. *Or at least to someone who needed to make a lot of fast getaways.*

Zak wondered what the interior looked like. If it was a smuggler ship, it would have all sorts of modifications, maybe even a high-powered weapons system. He looked over his shoulder to make sure he wasn't being watched, then slapped the hatch controls. The portal slid open with a soft hiss. Zak stepped onboard.

The first thing he noticed was the advanced computer system. The second thing he noticed was a long corridor leading to the cockpit.

The third thing he noticed was Dr. Evazan, the *dead* Dr. Evazan, running down the corridor toward him.

CHAPTER

Dr. Evazan was alive!

That was impossible. Boba Fett had shot him. Dr. Evazan had been buried. Zak had seen it with his own eyes.

But if Zak was going to believe what his eyes had seen last night, he had to believe them now. And right now his eyes told him that a dead man had come back to life and was charging toward him.

Zak was frozen in fear. Evazan's scarred face, his angry sneer, and his lightning speed were now even more terrifying. Zak could only stand there as Dr. Death reached out for him.

But instead of grabbing him, Evazan gave a sudden, violent twitch that shook his whole body. Then he snarled, shoved Zak out of the way, and bolted through the ship's hatchway, carrying something in his free hand. Evazan disappeared almost instantly as he ducked behind the landing gear of a nearby ship.

Finally Zak unfroze. He ignored the gangway ramp and leaped out of the starship. He hit the ground running and dashed across the dockyard to the others, shouting at the top of his lungs, "Evazan! Dr. Death! He's here. He's here!"

His frantic cries stopped Meego in midsentence. The salesman, along with Hoole, Tash, and Deevee, turned to look at the out-of-breath boy. "Ev-Evazan!" Zak gasped one more time.

"You are interrupting," Hoole said calmly. "Why?"

"I saw him. I saw Evazan."

"*The* Dr. Evazan?" Deevee asked.

Zak nodded. "Yes—scarred face and all."

Hoole looked annoyed. "If I recall correctly, this is the same Dr. Evazan who was buried today. In other words, the one who is dead?"

"He is! I mean he was! I mean . . ." Zak paused to catch his breath and saw the look on Tash's face. He realized that he must sound foolish. He tried to think of some way to prove what had happened.

"Perhaps I should excuse myself for a moment and let you four talk," the salesman said.

"No, wait!" Zak had just remembered something. "I saw Evazan running out of that ship back there. He was carrying something! Look over the ship and I'm sure you'll find something missing."

The salesman smiled in sympathy but said, "I'm afraid I can't help. You see, the reason that ship is unavailable is that it hasn't been overhauled yet. My technicians haven't even been inside, so I have no idea what might have been onboard."

No one spoke until they reached the hostel. They sat in the hostel's common room where they had seen Boba Fett the night before. But now the room was empty. Zak sat with his back to the wall, staring glumly out one of the small windows onto the darkening street.

The hostel was a cavernous place with high ceilings and stone pillars carved into the shape of giants holding up the roof. Their voices echoed so loudly that they found themselves whispering.

"Zak," Uncle Hoole began slowly. "I have tried to be understanding. I know that you have been having bad dreams about your parents, and that is quite understandable. But I believe your sudden concern about—forgive me for being so blunt—about *death* is becoming an obsession."

Zak knew arguing with Hoole wouldn't do any good. He tried to keep eye contact with his uncle, but the Shi'ido's stare made him nervous. Every now and then Zak looked away, out through the window to the dark streets beyond.

"We have hardly been here a full day and you've already offended a local custom by entering a cemetery. You've snuck out of your room with a boy who poisoned himself, and you have associated with a known bounty hunter."

Zak had stopped listening to his uncle. Had he seen something moving outside the window?

"Furthermore, you've become obsessed with this idea that the dead can return. I was fond of your parents, and I miss them, too, but you must accept that they are gone now. They cannot come back any more than this Dr. Evazan can."

Zak hardly heard what Hoole was saying. There was definitely something out in the shadows. It was a man-size shape. It shuffled one way, then the other, as if trying to get a good view of the room through the transparisteel. The figure pressed a little closer, and for a moment the light from the room spilled onto its face.

It was Dr. Evazan.

"There!" Zak shouted, pointing over Uncle Hoole's shoulder.

Everyone turned to look.

But Evazan had vanished.

"What?" Tash asked. "What was it?"

Zak opened his mouth, then shut it quickly. He

wasn't about to make any more claims in front of his uncle. "Nothing," he lied. "Just a shadow."

Zak could tell that Hoole didn't believe him. As he excused himself and went to his room, Zak decided that he couldn't blame his uncle or Deevee. But he at least hoped that Tash might believe him.

He told her so as they went to their rooms. "You're the expert on weird things," he told her. "Don't you think this really might be happening?"

"I believe that you believe it, Zak. But not even Jedi Knights can do what you're describing."

"But I know what I saw," Zak insisted. "Maybe Dr. Evazan faked his death so Boba Fett would stop tracking him."

"Maybe," Tash considered. "But it's pretty hard to fake your own burial after you're dead. He was put in a grave, remember?"

Zak nodded. "I know. But I did see him."

"I'm sure you saw someone, Zak. But it couldn't have been Dr. Evazan."

Zak knew Tash was right. It was impossible that Evazan could be alive. He had taken a blaster shot right in the back. Boba Fett had examined the corpse thoroughly, and the Necropolitans had put him in the ground.

Of course, it was just as impossible that zombies crawled out of their graves, but Zak had seen that, too.

Or had he?

Could he have imagined it? With all that mist and darkness, he hadn't actually gotten a good look at the zombies.

But what about Evazan? Hadn't he just seen Evazan's face at the window? Zak shuddered. The image was still in his mind. To make himself feel better, he hit the Lock button on his automatic window. The glass closed and sealed itself shut with a snap. The sound made Zak feel safe and secure.

He stood at his window and looked out on the twisted stone tops of the city buildings. Necropolis was a dark place. He had come to this planet already bothered by nightmares, and he had heard about nothing but graves and witches and cemeteries since the moment he arrived. Then, to make a friend so quickly and to have that friend taken away just as fast . . . maybe it was getting to him.

Someone had definitely been onboard the used starship. Zak didn't think he was *that* crazy. Maybe it was a thief. There were lots of criminals with scarred faces. Maybe Zak's fear had triggered something in his brain that made him see Evazan's face on someone else.

Zak lay down on his bed, staring at the ceiling, convincing himself that his imagination had been running overtime. Anyone would have the jitters after going through what he had experienced over the last twenty-four hours.

Tap. Tap. Tap.

The sudden, sharp raps shook the windowpane, and shook Zak even harder. He sat bolt upright.

In the window, a figure seemed to hang in midair. It was thin and bony, almost skeletal. Its jaw hung loosely from its head as it banged on the window again.

I'm dreaming, Zak thought. *I fell asleep on the bed while I was thinking, and now I'm having another nightmare.*

Tap. Tap. Tap.

The zombie acted just like those from his other dreams, moaning at him through the window. Zak didn't cry out. He wondered whether he was awake or dreaming.

The zombie started to pry the window open.

It must have been incredibly strong. Zak watched as it jammed its fingers into the tiny crack where the automatic window touched the stone wall. Somehow it found a hold and started to pull.

The window opened a fraction of a centimeter.

This must be a dream, Zak thought. *Not even a Wookiee could pry open those automatic windows.*

The zombie pulled, and the window opened a tiny bit wider.

Zak felt his heart start to pound.

The zombie pulled harder, its bony arms trembling under the strain. The automatic window started to whine as it tried to return to its closed position. The zombie pulled hard, and the window opened another centimeter. But that was all. With a demanding screech the automated window broke from the zombie's hand and slammed shut. The undead creature grunted and fell away from the window.

Heart still thumping in his chest, Zak waited a moment longer. Nothing else happened. He nodded to himself. That was the way to handle a nightmare.

He woke up the next morning feeling a little better. He was proud of the way he'd handled the nightmare. He hadn't given in to his fear; he hadn't cried out for help. He didn't know why the dream hadn't included his mom and dad, but maybe that was a good sign, too.

Zak yawned and stretched. His room was stuffy since he'd sealed the window shut. Rubbing the sleep from his eyes, Zak went to the window and pressed a button. The glass whooshed open.

Then Zak saw it.

Three small strips of pale dead skin clung to the edge of the window.

It hadn't been a dream. A zombie had tried to break into his room, and he had just lain there!

Zak shuddered, trying not to think about what might have happened if the undead creature had gotten inside. Worse yet, he wondered *why* the zombie had come after him in the first place.

But he knew the answer.

He had gone into the cemetery and stood on a grave.

He had disturbed the dead.

Zak didn't know what to do. He had already tried to tell Tash. He knew it wouldn't do any good to tell Uncle Hoole. Who could he talk to that might believe him?

Zak went to the comm unit built into his room wall.

Necropolis might have the look of an ancient city, but it possessed all the conveniences of modern galactic life. He punched up an information system and found Pylum's calling code, which he entered into the unit.

"Yes?" He heard Pylum's stern voice break through the static, and then a small image of the Necropolitan's face appeared on the comm unit's screen.

"Um, hello, my name is Zak. I was the one from the cemetery the other night . . ."

"Of course." Pylum's voice and face hardened. "The offworlder who violated our cemetery." He waited.

"I think . . . I think I know what you mean about the Curse of Sycorax." Zak swallowed. As calmly as he could, he reminded the Master of Cerements of what he'd seen in the graveyard. Then he told Pylum about the undead creature at his window and, finally, about the visit to the shipyard.

Pylum raised an eyebrow. "You believe you saw Dr. Evazan? The being that bounty hunter killed?"

"Yes," Zak said. Did Pylum believe him? "I saw him twice. Could he . . . Could he have come back, too?"

Pylum sounded upset. "The Curse of Sycorax knows no boundaries. Anything is possible. But this seems quite serious."

Zak was relieved. Someone finally believed him! Even if it *was* Pylum. "Can you help me? What should I do?"

"I will help you," Pylum replied, "but I must prepare. The ancient curse is not a thing to be taken lightly. I will send someone to you this evening. In the meantime it might be better if you kept this to yourself. Have you told anyone?"

"My sister, but she didn't believe me."

Pylum nodded. "Unbelievers are the most dangerous, because they cause problems without helping to solve them." The Master of Cerements paused. "I'm glad you've realized the truth, Zak. I believe I can help you, but it's important that you keep what you've seen to yourself. If word spreads it could cause a panic in the city. As Master of Cerements, I must know for certain what has happened before I make an announcement. Wait there. I will send someone." Pylum touched a button, and the screen went dark.

Zak spent the day on pins and needles. There was nothing to do—the boys he had met were all in mourning over Kairn, so there was no one to show him around the city. Uncle Hoole had apparently decided to buy the sleek new starship the slick dealer had pushed on him, and spent the day arranging the data work.

And Tash seemed preoccupied with Uncle Hoole himself. At first Zak was too distracted to pay attention, but by the afternoon, with nothing better to do but sit in the hostel and watch old holograms, Zak went to her room and listened as she told him about Hoole's meeting with Boba Fett.

"But Hoole's an anthropologist," Zak replied. "He's a scientist. What would he want from a bounty hunter?"

Tash shook her head. "I don't know. But there's definitely more to our uncle than meets the eye. And we're going to find out what it is."

"How are you going to find out?" Zak asked. "Uncle Hoole won't even tell us his first name."

It was true. But Tash only shrugged. "I'm not going to ask Uncle Hoole. I have another plan."

Boba Fett's ship was not hard to find. The maintenance workers at the dockyard had all gotten a glimpse of the intimidating killer, and knew exactly where his ship was. It sat on its landing berth like a poisonous dinko ready to spring. The ship's engines hummed. When they had first arrived, Tash thought the bounty hunter was about to launch, but that had been almost an hour ago. She figured that Fett always kept his ship primed for launch, just in case he had to make a quick getaway.

Her plan was simple. Since she couldn't ask Uncle Hoole, and she knew she couldn't ask Boba Fett, she would follow the bounty hunter to see what he was doing.

"If he ever comes out of his ship," she muttered to herself.

She lurked in the shadows of a building near the docking bay, where she could see the bounty hunter's ship. Beside her, Zak was growing anxious. Pylum had said he would send someone to the hostel, and evening had begun to fall. He was beginning to think that either the bounty hunter was not on board, or he never planned to leave his ship.

Zak became impatient. He didn't care about Boba Fett, and he had more important things to do than to discover Hoole's personal secrets. He decided he had to get back to the hostel so he could meet Pylum. "Tash," he began, "I—"

"Shh! There he is!"

The hatchway to the ship had opened. For a second no one appeared, as though the occupant was scanning for any lurking danger. Finally Boba Fett exited from the ship and strode down one of the numerous alleyways.

"Come on!" Tash whispered, and took off after the bounty hunter. Reluctantly Zak followed.

The alleyway curved into one of the city's main

streets. Turning onto it, Boba Fett walked in a straight line down the middle of the avenue. People got out of his way.

Zak and Tash followed as stealthily as they could. Even though it was getting late, there were still a few pedestrians on the street, and it was easy for Zak and Tash to remain out of sight as they followed their target. Boba Fett never looked back. He seemed unaware that he was being followed. Still, Tash thought they should take no chances. They dashed from hiding places behind pillars to covered doorways set in the sides of buildings, trying to remain as invisible as possible as they shadowed the bounty hunter.

After a few minutes, they reached a quieter section of town. There were no pedestrians at all. Zak recognized the neighborhood right away. They were getting closer to the cemetery.

The alleyways became as tight and narrow as a maze, and Zak and Tash soon lost sight of the bounty hunter as he turned a corner.

They hurried to catch up, but as they turned the same corner, they found themselves at an intersection of two streets. There was no sign of Boba Fett.

"Which way do you think he went?" Zak wondered.

"Your guess is as good as mine," Tash answered. "Why don't you take a quick look down that road, and I'll look down the other one. Then we'll meet back here in a minute."

Zak hesitated. He had to get back to the hostel. "Tash, I—"

"Come on, Zak!" Tash interrupted. "We might lose him."

She hurried down one of the two streets. Zak shook his head. When Tash locked onto something, she was as stubborn as a dewback.

He hurried down the avenue on the left. He hadn't gone far before the street divided again. Zak was at a loss until a figure passed beneath a faint glowpanel farther down one of the two lanes.

Quietly Zak hurried after the figure. He wondered if Boba Fett would even speak to him, or what the bounty hunter would say if he knew the man he'd killed had come back to life.

The figure ahead of him was moving slowly, and Zak easily closed the distance between them. He closed the gap just as the figure passed beneath another glowpanel, and Zak got a better look at him.

It wasn't Boba Fett.

It was Kairn.

Meanwhile Tash hurried down her chosen lane for two hundred meters. There were no side streets and no sign of Boba Fett. She decided he must not have come this way and turned back. She arrived back at the intersection and waited, but Zak didn't show up. She waited a little longer, then called softly, "Zak? Zak, are you there?"

"Zak is not here, but I am."

Tash turned. Boba Fett was behind her, with a blaster in his hand.

CHAPTER

"What did you do with Zak?" Tash demanded.

"You were following me," the bounty hunter stated. "Why?"

Maybe it was his voice, maybe it was the blaster in his hand, or maybe it was the fact that his face was hidden beneath his helmet, but Tash found Boba Fett unnerving. She stammered, "B-Because I saw you at the hostel the other day. T-Talking to my uncle."

"The Shi'ido," Fett stated flatly.

"Yes. I know he spoke to you, but he wouldn't tell me why. I wanted to find out by following you."

Boba Fett said flatly, "You were clumsy. I was on to you the minute I left my ship. Your clumsiness saved your life. If you had any skill at shadowing people, I might have mistaken you for a professional and taken you out immediately." He slowly holstered his blaster. "I expected your brother to be with you. I want him."

Tash tried to overcome her fear. *Boba Fett uses his reputation to intimidate people,* she thought. *And he uses that helmet to hide what he's thinking.*

"We split up," she said, keeping the nervousness out of her voice. "We lost you and separated to find you."

The cold voice spoke again. "I hear your brother says he saw Evazan again. Explain."

Tash was surprised. "How did you know that?"

"Explain."

Tash swallowed. Was Boba Fett angry at Zak? Did he think Zak would hurt his reputation? "Leave Zak alone. Whatever he says is our business."

"I want details. I killed Evazan. How could your brother have seen him?"

Tash gathered her courage. The bounty hunter had asked her a question, and it gave her an advantage. She had information he apparently needed. "Let's make a deal. I'll tell you what Zak saw, if you answer a question of mine."

"No promises. Tell me."

"Promise," she challenged.

The bounty hunter said nothing. He waited.

Tash tried to outwait him, but it was impossible. Boba Fett was like a statue. Finally she blurted out, "All right, I'll tell you!"

Tash quickly told the bounty hunter what Zak had seen aboard the starship. When she was finished, Fett simply nodded.

"Now I get to ask a question," Tash asked.

"It will be a waste of breath."

Tash asked anyway. "What does Uncle Hoole want from you? Does he want you to kill someone?"

"Stay out of your uncle's business. You don't want to know about it." The killer paused. "And if you know what's good for you, you'll stay out of my business as well."

Boba Fett pressed a small control on his wrist and the jetpack he wore ignited in a burst of flame. With a roar, the bounty hunter shot up into the air and was out of sight, leaving Tash alone on the dark street.

Zak rubbed his eyes and looked again. The person walking down the street was definitely the same boy he'd met his first day in Necropolis.

"Kairn!" Zak yelled happily. "You're alive!"

Kairn didn't stop moving, so Zak ran to catch up with him. Only when Zak stood right in front of him did the young Necropolitan seem to notice. "Kairn, it's me. Zak."

Kairn blinked. His skin was pale, as though he'd been very ill, and his eyes looked glassy and lifeless. They reminded Zak of black holes.

"Zak," Kairn said slowly. "Good to see you."

"It's good to see *you*! What happened? Was it all a mistake?"

Kairn blinked very slowly. "Mistake?"

Zak laughed. He was so happy to see his friend. "You were dead, or at least you looked dead. The other night in the cemetery, remember?"

"Oh. No. There was no mistake."

"You mean—?"

Kairn smiled a lifeless smile. "That's right. I died, Zak. I was dead." Kairn's body twitched.

Zak sputtered, "Then, it really is true? The dead can come back? But how?"

"I can answer your questions if you come with me. I must go to the graveyard again."

Kairn started walking down the street.

Zak didn't know what to do. He knew he should go back and meet Tash. He also knew Pylum had expected him to wait at the hostel. But if he left now, he might lose Kairn, and he refused to let that happen. If he was going to get anyone to believe him, he needed proof—and now his proof was walking away. Zak hurried until he was shoulder to shoulder with Kairn. "I'm right with you."

Kairn said nothing as they walked. Whatever had happened had definitely changed him. His skin looked sallow and unhealthy. He walked slowly, like he was trudging through mud, and every now and then his body shook with a violent twitch. But he didn't look

88

like the zombies Zak had seen in his dreams. He looked like he'd been ill, but he did not look like the walking dead.

Kairn's personality had changed along with his appearance. He didn't speak unless Zak asked him a question, and even then Zak had to ask it two or three times. It seemed as if Kairn's brain were in a fog as thick as the Necropolis night.

Still, all of those things paled in comparison to the miraculous fact that the dead young man was walking the streets of Necropolis!

When they reached the gates of the cemetery, Zak stopped. "I'm not sure I can go in there."

"I must go," Kairn said. "Inside here is the reason I came back."

"It's true then, isn't it?" Zak guessed. "There's something about the Crypt of the Ancients that brings back the dead."

"Yes."

Zak swallowed hard. "Kairn, this power, can it . . . Can it return anyone? From anywhere?"

Kairn smiled. "Come with me and see for yourself."

It sounded like another dare. Zak wouldn't have accepted it from anyone else, but Kairn was proof that some mystical power surrounded the crypt. He thought of his parents and decided it was a risk worth taking.

Kairn led him back through the graveyard until they

reached the massive Crypt of the Ancients. It looked the same as it had the other night.

Zak was impressed when Kairn grabbed the handles of the heavy doors in his thin, bony hands. The doors must have weighed several hundred kilos, but Kairn pulled them open easily. Beyond, a stairway led down into the dark.

"This is the way to the secret," Kairn said. "If you follow, you will see how the dead can come back to life."

"Um . . . okay," Zak said, suddenly feeling chilled.

He stepped inside behind Kairn, who paused only to slam the doors closed. Instantly they were plunged into utter darkness. Zak could not see Kairn, even though he was standing right next to him.

"Wait, it's too dark to go down there," Zak stated nervously.

"Oh, you need light. I forgot," Kairn replied. "Do you still have the glowrod I gave you?"

Zak fumbled in his pocket until he found the small rod and ignited it. It cast a faint light on the stone walls of the crypt.

Zak's pulse raced as they made their way down the steep, slippery stairs that curved into the ground. The stairs were so small that Zak kept one hand touching the stone wall beside him to keep his balance. Kairn didn't even have any problems getting down the stairs, though he was twitching violently.

Zak had seen that twitch in the graveyard zombies. He also had the feeling that he'd seen it somewhere else. Where had it been?

They reached the bottom of the spiral stairway and entered a small tomb. A great stone coffin lay in the center of the room. There were cobwebs all across its top, and a thick layer of dust lay on the floor around it. But next to the great coffin a pathway had been cleared of dust. This pathway led to another door at the far end of the tomb. Someone had used it often.

Kairn, still twitching, walked over and grabbed that door by a large metal handle. As he pulled the door open, Zak said, "It's the legend of the witch's curse, isn't it? All the stories about people coming here to call their loved ones back to life—they're true. It can be done."

"Of course it can be done," replied the voice of Dr. Evazan.

CHAPTER

Zak didn't think about it. He turned to run. But before he could take a step, Kairn grabbed his arm. Kairn's skin was ice-cold, and his grip was unbreakable.

"No, no, no," Dr. Evazan said in a sickly sweet voice. "You can't leave just as the fun is about to begin. Bring him here!"

Obediently Kairn dragged Zak further into the room. Zak struggled every step of the way, but Kairn had supernatural strength.

Evazan waited patiently until Zak stood before him. Kairn stood behind Zak, holding him by both shoulders. Zak continued to struggle, but he might as well have been fighting a stone.

"Welcome to my medical facility," Dr. Evazan began.

The crypt looked more like a chamber of horrors. The walls were lined with specimen jars full of squishy objects Zak didn't want to think about. Nearby stood a table covered with dull, rusty medical tools. There were several small doors along the back wall. Each door had a small barred window set in it, and through the window Zak could see pale zombies in the cells. He looked at Evazan again and shuddered. "You're supposed to be dead."

Evazan chuckled. "True. But I'm the doctor, so I get to announce the time of death. And my time hasn't come yet. Or I should say, it's come and gone, and I'm still here."

Evazan twitched and Zak remembered—he had seen Evazan twitch onboard the starship!

"What do you mean?" Zak asked.

Evazan pretended to be surprised. "You mean you haven't figured it out yet? Doesn't your friend Kairn here give you any hints at all?" Evazan threw his arm back in a sweeping gesture that covered the entire room. "I've had a breakthrough in my experiments. I have figured out a way to reanimate dead tissue."

"What does that mean?" Zak asked.

"It means," Evazan said triumphantly, "I have learned to bring back the dead. Like I did with your friend Kairn here. And myself, of course."

Zak felt fear and relief churn in his stomach. Dr. Evazan was a mad scientist, but at least now Zak knew he wasn't insane. "How could you bring yourself back if you were dead in the first place?"

Evazan laughed, and the unscarred side of his face wrinkled into a horrific grin. "In my line of work, it's good to think ahead. I heard that Boba Fett was in the area, and I knew he'd find me eventually. I injected myself with the reanimation serum. Once I died, there was only one step left in the process before I came back."

"And those zombies in the cages back there. They're like the ones I saw earlier. They're more of your experiments?"

"My, my, you ask a lot of questions. But I suppose it's good for me to practice my bedside manner. People say it's my weak point." Evazan began to fill a syringe with a pale red liquid. "Your timing at the cemetery was extraordinary. You got to see some of my undead creatures come alive, so to speak. Of course, those are the cruder models. They look more dead than alive."

"But you and Kairn look . . ."

"Alive?" Evazan gloated. "That is due to my genius. I've made improvements since my first experiments. My new zombies look a bit healthier, and they can talk. My tests indicate they even keep their old memories. Kairn is a good example of the next stage and well, frankly, so am I."

Dr. Death actually looked sad for a moment. "The

unfortunate thing is that I couldn't use the improved serum on the rest of the corpses in the graveyard. I'm afraid I need fresh bodies for it to work properly. Old bodies come out clumsy and awkward. For the results to be perfect, I have to be the one to kill my patients. That's why I force-fed your friend here the crypt-berries. They killed him without doing too much damage."

Zak was horrified. "You mean you killed him just so you could bring him back to life?"

"Of course." Evazan held up the syringe and looked at Kairn. "Kairn, put your friend on the table."

"Kairn, don't do it! Help me!" Zak said.

For the slightest moment, Kairn paused.

"Oh, I'd save what little breath I had left, if I were you," Evazan warned. "These zombies listen only to *my* commands. Put him on the table."

This time Kairn obeyed immediately. He lifted Zak easily and dropped him on the examining table. The undead Necropolitan pinned him down with a viselike grip. "But why are you doing this—why are you creating zombies?" Zak managed to ask.

Evazan held up the syringe and squeezed it until one drop of the pale red liquid bubbled out and ran down along the edge of the needle. "Haven't you noticed how strong they are? Also, they don't feel any pain at all, and they are easily conditioned to take orders. In other words, they'll make perfect soldiers. And since

people are always dying, there will be a limitless supply." Evazan seemed horribly pleased with himself.
"Whoever uses my process will have an inexhaustible,
invincible army. And I, of course, will become very
rich."

"You're insane! Who would buy this serum?"

"Oh, I already have a buyer. A very, very powerful
buyer. He's close to the Emperor himself, I believe."
Evazan twitched violently. He saw Zak staring at him
and shrugged through another twitch. "The twitching
is a defect in the serum. But I think I've fixed it. I'll
know as soon as my next subject reanimates."

"Your next subject?"

Evazan looked surprised. "Why, yes. You, of
course."

He brought the needle close to Zak.

"No!" Zak struggled against Kairn's impossible
grip. "Kairn! We were friends!"

Kairn spoke slowly. "I'm sorry, Zak." He twitched,
and Zak thought he felt Kairn's grip loosen.

"Silence!" Evazan snarled. "I didn't give you per-
mission to speak. Now hold him still!"

Instantly Kairn's grip grew tight again. Evazan
mumbled, "Interesting. This new version of zombie is
less obedient than the earlier ones. I'll have to take
care of that."

Evazan poked the needle into Zak's arm.

Zak kicked and thrashed, trying to free himself, but Kairn was far too strong.

"Seeing as how you should be my greatest success, it's only fair to tell you about the process itself. It's quite brilliant. The serum contains most of the active ingredients. The only thing missing is the final chemical—oddly enough, it's a chemical found in the slime trails of the boneworms that live on Necropolis."

"So that's why you're working here."

"Exactly. All I have to do is dig up the body, or get to it before it's buried, and inject the serum. Once the body is back in the ground, I simply let the boneworms do their work."

"But the boneworms *eat* the bodies," Zak said with a shudder.

"No, no, no," Dr. Evazan corrected. "The boneworms dig their way into the skin and suck the marrow from your bones. Once they've had their fill, my serum kicks in, filling the bones with reanimation fluid. It's absolutely brilliant." Evazan checked his chronometer. "And it's just a matter of time before my latest batch of undead scratch and claw their way to the surface."

Zak's arm throbbed where Evazan had given him the shot. He was surprised when Dr. Death picked up another needle, this one full of clear liquid.

"Another shot?" Zak moaned. He was already feeling ill.

"Oh, that first shot wasn't the serum. That was a diluted version of cryptberry juice. Instead of killing you like normal cryptberry juice does, that shot will put you into a coma. Of course, everyone will think you're dead. *This* is the reanimation serum."

Evazan jabbed the second needle into Zak's arm.

The doctor nodded matter-of-factly. "You see, I think the twitching is a side effect of the original death, like the blaster shot that killed me or the poison that killed Kairn here. So instead of killing you in a conventional way, I'm giving you the serum first. Then I'm going to, shall we say, extinguish your flame in the way that will do the least damage."

Zak felt himself growing drowsy. "Wh-what are you going to do."

"Oh, I'm not going to do anything," Evazan said with the cruelest of smiles. "I'm going to let your friends do it for me."

Zak woke from the first restful sleep he'd had in several nights. He had not had a single nightmare, not even a dream. His first waking thought was that he felt refreshed.

He tried to open his eyes but couldn't. He tried to sit up, but he couldn't. When he tried to move his arms, his hands, even his fingers, nothing happened. He was completely paralyzed.

He still had his sense of touch. He could tell that he

was lying down on something soft and warm. Was he in his own bed?

He heard someone crying nearby. It was Tash. Then he heard Deevee's voice.

"That's right, Tash," the droid was saying awkwardly. "Let it out. It's no shame to cry when a loved one passes on."

Loved one? Who had died? Zak wondered if something terrible had happened to Uncle Hoole. But then he heard Uncle Hoole's voice. "They're ready to begin now, Tash."

What's going on? Why can't I move?

He heard Tash sob. "Oh, Zak, what happened to you? You knew those cryptberries were dangerous. How could this have happened?"

What? Zak wanted to yell. But he couldn't speak.

Uncle Hoole spoke again. "Step back now, Tash. At least the Necropolitans have allowed us to say goodbye to Zak. It goes against their customs to let mourners be so close to the grave. Come now. They're ready for the burial."

Burial?

Zak heard a heavy lid close right over his head, and he sensed that he was now in a small, confined space. A cold feeling settled in his stomach as he realized that it was a coffin.

He was inside a *coffin*.

They were going to bury him alive.

CHAPTER 14

From inside the coffin, Zak tried to shout "I'm alive! I'm alive!" But his mouth wouldn't move. He was still under the influence of the paralyzing cryptberry juice.

He heard someone begin to speak outside. It was Pylum, the Master of Cerements. Pylum began to repeat the same funeral rites he had said over Kairn's grave.

I don't need a funeral! I'm not dead! I'm not dead! Zak cried. No one heard him. His screams were all in his head.

Pylum finished the funeral rites and added a speech, which he directed to those who had gathered. "It is a tragedy when any young person passes on. It is especially sad that an offworlder has gone into the void. But let the living learn a lesson from the passing of

Zak Arranda. He was a good young man, but he disturbed the graves of the dead, and for that he paid the ultimate price."

There is no curse! It was Evazan! He's come back! He did this to me!

Pylum continued. "We dedicate this ground to the memory of the dearly departed Zak Arranda. Let all honor be bestowed upon the dead. Let the dead rest with the dead as long as the galaxy spins. Let this ground remain sealed over the departed forever and ever."

No!

Zak heard a heavy bolt slam into place, just like the one he'd seen on Kairn's coffin. He was locked inside.

Forever.

Zak felt himself being lowered into a hole. He heard Tash sob one more time. Then there was a loud thump on top of the coffin.

They were shoveling dirt over him.

Zak had a terrible thought. Maybe he *was* dead. Maybe Evazan had given him too much cryptberry juice and had killed him. Could this be what death was like, to be frozen forever in one place?

As more clumps of dirt dropped onto the coffin, Zak imagined the hours turning into days, the days turning into weeks, the weeks into years. After hundreds of years, would he still be here, stuck in this same dark hole for all time?

The sound of shoveling had grown quieter. Dark thoughts crept into Zak's brain. There was no use in struggling. Just accept your fate. Your life is over.

Zak imagined his parents. He had wanted to see them again, to say goodbye to them. Now he knew that was useless. What little was left of them floated among the space debris that had once been Alderaan. Frozen, unreachable, untouchable.

Memories filled Zak's mind: picnics with his parents and Tash, riding a hoverboat on the lake, playing two-person touchball. He remembered the day his father had taught him to ride a skimboard.

Eager to remember everything about his parents, Zak tried to recall every moment he could, right up to the last one. Six months ago he and Tash had packed their things to go on a two-week field trip. It was their first time away from home, and they were both a little nervous. Zak remembered telling his parents how scared he was.

"I've never been so far away from you before," he had said.

His mother had hugged him. "Don't worry, Zak. You could be on the other side of the galaxy, but you're always right here in my heart, so you're never really far away. And as long as you keep me there, I'll be near to you, too."

Zak had forgotten those words until that moment.

His mother had told him to keep her in his heart. He hadn't done that. He'd been too busy feeling depressed to think of all the good times he'd had with them, to keep his memories of them alive.

That's where I should have looked for them, Zak decided. *Instead of searching in old superstitions, I should have looked inside me. That's where mom and dad are. That's where they'll always be!*

But he had realized it too late. Zak blinked as he felt a tear sting his eye.

I blinked!

Zak felt his mouth move. He opened it and closed it experimentally. Then he tried to move his hand. His fingers moved. He wiggled his toes. He couldn't move his arms or legs yet, but the cryptberry drug was wearing off.

If the drug is wearing off, that means I'm alive. I really am alive!

Hope surged in Zak. If he was alive, there had to be something he could do. He filled his lungs with air and shouted "I'm alive! Somebody help me! I'm alive!"

He wondered if the sound would reach up through the ground. He hoped it would. Now that he knew he was alive, he was desperate to get out of the coffin. He would soon run out of air.

"Help! Someone get me out of here!"

Seconds later Zak heard a small scraping noise

against the lid of his coffin. At first he thought some-one had heard him already, but then he heard a similar noise beneath him.

Then he heard the sound on both sides of his coffin. Zak realized what it was.

The boneworms were gnawing their way in.

CHAPTER 15

Tash, Deevee, and Uncle Hoole walked slowly back to the hostel as another dark Necropolitan day faded to an even darker night.

Tash was devastated. Zak's death had been a terrible shock to them all.

After her encounter with Boba Fett, Tash had turned back to look for Zak. She soon realized that it was impossible to find anyone among the winding streets of the dark city. She assumed that he'd just gotten bored, or lost, and would make his way back to the hostel as soon as he could.

At the hostel she had waited for an hour, and Zak still hadn't returned. She began to get a heavy, sinking feeling, as though a black hole had opened in her stomach. It was a feeling she'd had before—the feeling that something was terribly wrong. Despite her feeling, she was at first afraid to tell Uncle Hoole, because she didn't want to reveal the reason she and Zak had gone out. After all, they were spying on Boba Fett and trying to get information about Hoole himself.

But when another hour passed and the feeling of dread grew stronger, Tash knew she couldn't wait. She went to Uncle Hoole and told him that Zak was missing.

Hoole reacted in his usual stern Shi'ido way. "What was he doing out? That young man is constantly getting into trouble."

"Um, this time it was my fault, Uncle Hoole," Tash confessed. "I wanted to . . . um . . . see a few things, and I convinced him to go along. We got separated."

Uncle Hoole frowned. "Then we have you to thank for this disturbance. Come on, we had better summon the authorities."

Uncle Hoole convinced the owner of the hostel to help them, and soon they had called the local law enforcement. Zak's description was sent to all the local patrols, but because he had only been gone a few hours, the authorities wouldn't launch a full-fledged search.

Uncle Hoole decided that they should search the

streets themselves. "Tash, you will come with me. Deevee, you will search on your own. Can you manage?"

Deevee was a droid, but he had practiced long and hard to develop a very humanlike imitation of disgust. He sarcastically replied, "I have calculated the number of colored grains in a Tatooine sand painting. I think I can manage to walk and look for Zak at the same time."

Deevee quickly began searching for Zak. No matter what the droid said, he was fond of his two troublesome charges.

While Hoole and Tash had searched the streets, Deevee headed directly for one specific location. His computer brain had already formulated a theory, but the conclusion sent a tremor through his servos. Deevee ran his theory through his logic circuits for any sign of malfunction, but found none.

Deevee's analytical program was extremely sophisticated, and he was almost never wrong.

Which is why it was Deevee who had found Zak lying in the cemetery, with a few cryptberries still clutched in his hand.

Deevee had summoned help, and Zak had been rushed to a medical facility immediately, but it was too late. The cryptberries had done their work.

"It just doesn't make sense," Tash had said

tearfully as she, her uncle, and the droid reached the hostel. "Why would Zak do something like that? He knew those berries were poisonous."

Uncle Hoole put a hand on her shoulder, "Zak has been rather . . . distracted . . . lately. I can't say I know what he was thinking. We may never know."

Tash couldn't accept that. "That's not good enough for me, Uncle Hoole, and it shouldn't be good enough for you. Zak would never have eaten those berries on his own. Someone must have forced him, or tricked him. You can't really believe that Zak was the victim of some ancient curse of the dead!"

Uncle Hoole looked skeptical. "Who would have a reason to harm Zak?"

Tash shrugged. "Maybe Zak wasn't seeing things after all. Maybe this Dr. Evazan is still alive."

Uncle Hoole considered the possibility. "It is extremely unlikely, Tash."

But Tash's words sounded right to her, and she was learning to trust her intuition.

"You're a scientist," she challenged. "You shouldn't make up your mind until you have proof. And there's only one way to find out."

Hoole looked intrigued. "What do you propose?"

Tash decided to lay her cards on the table. "I want to dig up Dr. Evazan's grave. That's what Zak wanted to do, but I talked him out of it."

She was afraid that Hoole would refuse immediately. To her surprise, the Shi'ido contemplated her request for a long moment. Then he turned to Deevee. "Deevee, you have files on Necropolis. Is there any custom or law that permits the dead to be exhumed?"

Deevee scanned his internal files. "I'm afraid not, Master Hoole. On Necropolis, once the body is buried, that's where it stays. At least, that's where one hopes it stays."

Tash's heart sank. "Does that mean we can't have Evazan's grave dug up?"

"No," Uncle Hoole said firmly, "it means we will have to do it ourselves."

Tash jumped to her feet. "Uncle Hoole, really?"

"That is an excellent decision, Master Hoole!" Deevee said excitedly. Then he calmed his voice down. "Of course, it's my duty to warn you that grave-robbing is a serious offense on Necropolis. We must be careful."

The Shi'ido nodded. "I agree. That's why we must be ready to leave immediately. I want you to go back to the dockyard and see to the final arrangements about purchasing our new ship. Tash and I will meet you there."

A few kilometers away and two meters beneath the ground, Zak heard the scraping outside his coffin grow louder. He could move one of his arms now, and he fumbled awkwardly in his pocket. He hoped they

109

hadn't removed his possessions before burying him . . .

There! He still had the small glowrod that Kairn had given him that first night. He activated it now, shedding a gloomy light on his tiny prison.

He wondered how much oxygen he had left. The light of the glowrod revealed small holes in the coffin. Who would put holes in a coffin?

Evazan!

As Zak watched, slimy, white creatures began to force their long fat bodies through the openings.

The boneworms were coming in.

CHAPTER

16

Deevee arrived at the dockyard as nervous as a newly programmed protocol droid. Although he was pleased about Hoole's decision, he wondered why his master was taking such a great risk. It wasn't like Hoole to act irrationally. But sometimes the Shi'ido did things that even Deevee didn't understand.

The smiling salesman, Meego, greeted Deevee warmly. "Good evening. We were just about to close up for the night. How may I be of service?"

"I am here to see that the ship we purchased is ready to be picked up."

Meego's smile widened. "Ah, yes, your ship, your ship. Well, we've had a slight problem with your ship. Nothing serious, mind you, just a small curve in the hyperspace lane, so to speak."

Deevee was not programmed for metaphors. "A curve in a hyperspace lane would cause immense damage to anyone traveling there and probably result in a loss of life. Is that what you are implying, sir?"

The salesman winked as though he were telling a joke. "Look, it's not that bad. The truth is we, um, accidentally sold your ship to someone else. Can you believe it? Of all the foolish things! I can't tell you how sorry I am."

"What *can* you tell me?" the droid said. "Specifically, what can you tell me about the credits my master transferred to you."

Meego looked hurt. "Oh, not to worry, not to worry. Your master's credits are safe with Meego. We'll just consider them a down payment on any other ship you choose."

The droid's logic circuits sent out an internal alarm. "Down payment? You mean you expect us to give you *more* money because you made a mistake?"

Meego's expressive face sudden became very sympathetic. "Now, now, we are sorry about the error. But, you see, you bought the least expensive ship in the dockyard. So if you want to buy another one, you'll have to spend just a little bit more."

The salesman shrugged and smiled.

Deevee knew when he was being tricked. His analytical circuits burned hot as he searched for a solution. He looked around at the rows of ships until his photoreceptors settled on the well-worn hull of the ship Zak had told them about. It looked more like scrap metal than a starship, but Deevee trusted Zak's opinion. "What about that ship?"

The salesman frowned. "That ship? Oh, um, well, as I said the other day, that ship hasn't yet been overhauled. It's not for sale yet."

"But my master requires a ship immediately, and that is the only one we can buy with the money we've already paid."

The salesman shrugged. "Then I guess you'll have to make a down payment on a more expensive one."

Deevee accessed a particular memory file. "Sir, I was just thinking about the Tal Nami system."

"Really? What about it?" the salesman asked.

"The Tal Nami have a very interesting culture. Their bodies need two foods to survive—the fruit of the egoa tree and the root of the capabara plant. But the two plants can't grow in the same regions. So the Tal Nami of one region have to trade with the Tal Nami of another region for everyone to survive. In order to prevent the entire population from starving, they have developed a code of honor among traders. Each trader tries to make sure the *other* one gets the better end of the bargain. Since both sides are doing this, it assures a fair trade."

"Fascinating," the dealer yawned.

"Of course, any trader who is caught dealing unfairly is immediately punished. His feet are tied to the roots of an egoa tree, and his hands are tied to the branches of that same tree. The egoa tree grows at a rate of one meter per day. The result is gruesome, but the Tal Nami have an intense dislike of villainous traders. They will travel light-years to track one down." Deevee paused for effect. "Have you ever been to Tal Nami, sir?"

"Can't say that I have."

"Master Hoole has. Several times, to visit friends. Good friends. In fact I believe he plans to go there soon. I can only imagine what the Tal Nami would say if Master Hoole arrived in a ship foisted on him by an unscrupulous dealer."

Meego swallowed. "Did you say they'd travel light-years to track down . . ."

"Yes, sir," Deevee replied. "Light-years."

Meego stared at Deevee, but it was impossible to tell if the droid were bluffing or not. Finally he shook his head. "Suit yourself, droid. I'd probably never get rid of this heap anyway. People would be afraid to buy it."

"Why is that?" Deevee asked.

"Too much bad history," said the salesman. "Didn't I mention it before? This ship is called the *Shroud*. It used to belong to that criminal, Dr. Evazan."

Deevee opened the hatchway and let himself onboard. He was surprised at the sophisticated equipment inside. Evazan might have been an evil doctor, but he was obviously quite intelligent.

"Now you know I'm not supposed to do this," Meego said. "It's against regulations to sell used ships until the memory banks have been wiped. You never know what kind of personal information might get passed along."

"That's correct," Deevee said. "You never do know."

Deevee's sophisticated brain buzzed with theories. If this was Evazan's ship, maybe Zak *had* seen him onboard. Hadn't Zak said that Evazan was carrying something away with him? Perhaps Evazan had come back to get some important information. Deevee wondered if he'd gotten it all.

He punched up the computer. "Hey, you're not supposed to do that!" Meego protested.

Deevee looked at the salesman. "Do you recall the extra credits you tried to squeeze from me a few moments ago? Hand this ship over to me with the memory banks intact, and those credits are yours."

Meego had never been one to care much for regulations, especially when there was profit to be made. "It's a deal."

A few minutes later, Deevee was alone, browsing through a library full of computer files. Some had been deleted, but many more were intact. Deevee's photoreceptors skimmed across one startling title: "RE-ANIMATION OF DEAD TISSUE."

Urgent alarms rattled Deevee's program as he scanned the report. He was at first amazed at what he read—and then horrified as he saw the phrase "the use of cryptberries may enhance the reanimation process. They induce a state that imitates death, which will allow for further preparation of the body . . ."

A state that imitates death . . .

Deevee made the connection. "Zak!"

Deevee turned to go, but found his way was blocked.

Boba Fett had crept up behind him.

At the graveyard Tash and Uncle Hoole found the iron gates sealed shut. They could see the control panel on the inside wall through the bars, but it was much too far away for them to reach.

"Wait a moment," Uncle Hoole said.

He closed his eyes. His skin started to wriggle and squirm across his body like it was alive. Then Hoole's whole body began to twist and transform. In moments the Shi'ido had disappeared, and a Ranat—a small rat-like creature stood in its place. "I'll be right back," the Ranat said.

Hoole had shape-shifted as easily as most people walk or talk.

Hoole slipped easily through the bars and scampered over to the control panel inside the cemetery wall. The control panel was set too high for a Ranat to reach, so the Shi'ido shape-shifted again, and Hoole reappeared. He punched a few buttons, and the gates swung open.

Tash shook her head. "I'll never get used to that."

"It is an ability that is often useful," Hoole admitted. "Now we must hurry."

Dr. Evazan's grave was on the far side of the cemetery, in a plot reserved for criminals and Imperial bureaucrats. Tash and Uncle Hoole had brought two small shovels with them.

"You know, we *are* disturbing the dead." Tash smiled nervously. "They could get angry."

Hoole scowled. "Ridiculous. That is superstitious nonsense, Tash."

Tash didn't answer.

Hoole plunged his shovel into the ground. He scooped up a few shovelfuls of dirt, then noticed that Tash wasn't helping. He looked at his niece curiously. She had grown very pale. "Is something wrong, Tash?"

Tash tried to speak, but she couldn't. Her mouth was dry and her tongue had frozen. She pointed over Hoole's shoulder.

A zombie was staggering toward them.

CHAPTER

The undead creature had pale skin, stringy hair, and a sunken, skeletal face. It was exactly like the creatures Zak had described.

Uncle Hoole turned just as the zombie came within reach. Instinctively the Shi'ido threw up the shovel he was holding to ward off the ghoulish-looking creature. The shovel slammed against the zombie's head, but it didn't seem to notice. It grabbed Hoole with both arms and squeezed so hard that the scientist gasped.

"Uncle Hoole!" Tash cried, taking a step forward.

"Stay . . . back!" Hoole grunted. "It's too strong." Hoole felt the air being forced from his lungs. He took as deep a breath as he could, and closed his eyes. His entire body started to wriggle, and the zombie squeezed tighter. But Hoole was no longer there. The zombie found itself holding a slippery water eel that thrashed wildly until it shot from the undead monster's arms. It landed on the ground with a slap and shape-shifted back into Hoole. The zombie roared and lumbered forward once more.

"Tash, run!" Uncle Hoole ordered.

Tash didn't argue. She turned and started to run, but in front of her a grave suddenly broke open like a cracking egg. A clawing white hand reached out of the ground and ice-cold fingers wrapped themselves around her ankle. Tash stomped on the arm with her free foot, but the zombie was unaffected by pain. With its free hand, it continued to dig its way up from beneath the ground. Tash could see its dead face, still half-buried, leering up at her from the hole in the ground.

Uncle Hoole dropped to his knees beside her, using both hands to pry the zombie's fingers away from Tash. But the creature was incredibly strong, and even together they could not break its grip.

"What are we going to do?" Tash gasped.

Hoole tried to remain calm, but even he looked worried. "Try to use our heads," he answered.

Hoole stood up and turned to the other zombie, which was staggering toward them. The Shi'ido made himself an easy target, standing just to the side of Tash in front of the second zombie's grave. Growling, the first zombie lunged forward to grab him, but once again Hoole shape-shifted—into the tiny Ranat form he'd taken before. The lunging zombie stumbled right over him and fell headlong into the second grave. The two undead creatures both howled, struggling with each other, and Tash pulled her leg free.

Hoole, now back in his own shape, helped Tash to her feet and they started toward the exit.

"By the stars!" Uncle Hoole swore.

Tash was startled. She had never seen Uncle Hoole lose his composure. But in the next moment, she saw why.

All around them the ground was churning. Massive headstones collapsed or sank into the ground as the creatures below struggled to reach the surface. Hundreds of graves were on the verge of breaking open, spilling forth their buried inhabitants.

The city of the dead was coming back to life.

Tash and Uncle Hoole had no choice but to run through the mass of writhing graves.

At first their escape seemed easy. It took the zombies several minutes to dig their way to the surface.

Groping hands and arms snatched at Tash and Hoole from the graves. Tash shuddered—it looked like a horrible garden of fingers, arms, and hands planted in the ground.

Before long they could see figures rising up in the mist before them. Farther along, the zombies had had more time to free themselves, and between them and the gates lay an army of the undead.

"Zak was right!" Tash yelled to Hoole. "The dead are coming back! How can this be?"

Hoole panted for breath as he ran. "I don't know. Yet."

They plunged into the mist.

The zombies were relentless and incredibly strong, but they were slow. Twitching and staggering, they closed in on their two targets. Uncle Hoole and Tash slipped away from them or ducked under their arms. To Tash it seemed like some twisted version of the games of touchball she and Zak had played with their parents at home.

Tash was tall for her age, but she was limber and quick and able to dodge the pursuing creatures. Twice Hoole was grabbed, and twice he shape-shifted out of the zombies' clutches. But more and more zombies came after them out of the mist, and escape looked impossible until they saw a row of iron bars before them.

"The gates!" Uncle Hoole said. "We've made it!"

Tash gasped as a zombie nearly grabbed her by the neck. She slipped away and dashed for the gate, followed closely by her uncle.

The gates were ajar, and they slipped through, slamming the doors behind them. Zombies surged toward the gates, pulling at the iron bars.

Tash and Hoole had escaped the cemetery. They didn't wait to see if the gate would hold the zombies back. They ran headlong down one of the city's cobblestoned avenues. Only when they were far from the graveyard did they pause to catch their breath.

Tash's heart still had not stopped pounding when the noise of a crowd reached her ears. People, many people, were surging toward them from a nearby street. Angry words were shouted in their direction.

"What's going on?" she asked.

Hoole frowned. "That is a mob. And Pylum is leading it."

The Master of Cerements led the mob right to Hoole and Tash. As they approached, Hoole shouted, "This place isn't safe! Something terrible is happening at the cemetery. Corpses are coming back to life."

Pylum scowled and jabbed a bony finger their way. "We know. And it's all your fault!"

CHAPTER

18

Pylum's eyes glinted angrily. "The dead are rising all over the city! Corpses walk the streets. People are fleeing in terror. And you caused it!" The angry mob shouted its agreement with Pylum.

"We didn't do anything!" Tash protested.

The Master of Cerements pointed to the cemetery. "Your brother offended the dead by entering the cemetery, and now you two have followed him. You have brought the Curse of Sycorax down on our heads."

Hoole shook his head. "There has to be a more reasonable explanation for this than some ancient curse. I'm sure we can find a solution for this problem if we work together."

"See, see!" Pylum screeched, turning to the mob of Necropolitans. "They ignore our ancient laws! They trample our sacred ground. I warned you that this might happen, and now it has!"

"What can we do?" one of the Necropolitans pleaded. "Pylum, please help us."

Pylum raised himself up to his full height and proclaimed, "I am the Master of Cerements. I have read the ancient laws. The dead will not be appeased until the offenders have been punished. They must be taken to the Crypt of the Ancients!"

"Wait!" Hoole yelled in a commanding voice. "You can't possibly believe that we are responsible for this. We must work together!"

But his words were drowned out by the cries of the mob. The Necropolitans swarmed around them, surrounding Tash and grabbing Hoole. For a moment Tash thought the Shi'ido would shape-shift into a Wookiee or some other ferocious being and fight his way to safety, but he did nothing. She added that to the growing list of mysteries that surrounded Hoole.

Pylum led the mob and the two prisoners back to the cemetery. They found that the twisted gates had been wrenched from their settings and tossed to the ground. The zombies were nowhere in sight, but Tash didn't want to take chances. "You don't want to go in there," she said to Pylum, "trust me."

The Master of Cerements scowled. "You fool. The dead have already risen. They are terrorizing the city. The graveyard is empty."

It was true. The cemetery had become a wide field of empty holes and mounds of earth. The long rows of headstones had toppled. In most places the soil had been trampled and churned to mud by the passage of the undead. It was eerily quiet.

The angry Necropolitans paused at the bizarre sight of so many upturned graves. Some of them cried out and wept.

"See what the offworlders have caused," the Master of Cerements screeched. "Bring them to the crypt!"

Urged on by Pylum, the Necropolitans dragged Hoole and Tash across the field of empty graves, toward the center of the cemetery. There, the massive Crypt of the Ancients still stood as solemn and ominous as ever.

"Open the doors!" Pylum ordered.

Some of the Necropolitans gasped. "But we've never opened up the crypt before!"

The Master of Cerements held up his hand to silence them. "These are cursed times. The ancient laws demand that we throw the violators into the crypt. Open the doors!"

Tash was amazed at how willingly the mob followed Pylum's orders. Only a few days ago, some of them had thought he was an old fool fretting about outdated superstitions. Now they were frightened enough to make him their leader.

It took two or three strong men pulling at each handle, and even then the great doors moved reluctantly. When the doors were opened wide enough, Pylum ordered them to stop. "Put the offworlders inside."

Tash and Hoole were shoved through the opening so roughly that Tash would have tumbled down the steep stairway if Hoole hadn't caught her arm. They turned back toward the opening, where they could see Pylum addressing the mob. "Go back to your homes! I will go into the crypt and plead with Sycorax to call off this evil curse. When I enter, shut the doors behind me and go back to your homes until all is calm again!"

With that, Pylum entered the crypt. The Necropolitans shut the doors behind him, plunging all three of them into complete darkness.

A second later there was small click and a glowrod lit up the stairwell, casting eerie light over Pylum's face. He looked at Tash and Hoole, and chuckled.

"Those superstitious fools," he laughed.

"What?" Tash replied in amazement.

Pylum laughed again. "Imagine believing all that nonsense about curses and legends."

"Y-You mean you don't?" she stuttered.

"Of course not." Pylum pushed past them and started down the stairs. "Follow me."

Tash and Hoole had no choice but to follow Pylum down the steep stairway into the tomb below. At the bottom of the stairs, Tash could see two stone coffins and a large, closed door. Pylum walked up to the coffins.

"Sycorax," he chuckled. "What a foolish story. But at least all my years of study finally proved useful."

"I don't know what you're thinking, Pylum," Uncle Hoole said, "but I warn you that you alone are no match for me."

Pylum grinned. "Oh, I know all about your Shi'ido powers. You could turn into a wampa ice beast and tear me apart right here. In fact that's why I arranged to have you brought down here. My associates and I consider your shape-changing powers a perfect test."

Tash's brain was spinning in confusion. "Test of what?"

Pylum smiled. "Why, a test of our undead soldiers, naturally."

He pounded on the door. It slowly creaked open.

Inside an army of zombies was waiting.

CHAPTER

Tash screamed.

Hoole didn't hesitate. In the blink of an eye, he did exactly as Pylum predicted. He quickly shape-shifted into an enormous wampa ice beast, using the creature's great claws to swipe at the zombies. His blows tossed them aside like feathers. But after every blow, the zombies simply stood up and started forward again, clutching at his arms and legs.

Tash knew she could do nothing to stop the zombies. But she thought she could slow them down. She found an old length of chain lying on the tomb floor and used it to trip the awkward zombies. It didn't slow them for long, but at least it kept some of them from swarming over Hoole.

The Shi'ido shifted from a wampa to a gundark and from a gundark to a reptilian creature that Tash had never seen before, but nothing stopped the undead. They felt no pain and no fear, and they were determined to bring Hoole down.

Hoole and Tash soon found themselves backed up against the wall. Zombies crowded into the small space around them, pressing forward. Hoole had transformed into a Wookiee, and shoved the zombies back with a roar, but it was like pushing against a brick wall. Powerful hands clutched at his Wookiee fur, dragging him down and smothering him.

In a blur, Hoole transformed into a dozen different species from across the galaxy. But none of them were strong enough, fast enough, or slippery enough to escape the undead mob. Hoole returned to his Wookiee form for one last surge of strength, then fell to his knees with a defiant roar. A dozen zombies hung onto him, ensuring that he could not get up again. Hoole had lost the battle.

Pylum drew a small blaster from his pouch and held it to Tash's head. "Now, Dr. Hoole, I suggest you return to your normal shape and stay that way before I do the girl serious harm."

The Wookiee snarled but obeyed. Hoole reappeared under the pile of walking corpses. He looked tired but unhurt.

Beyond the door, Tash heard the sound of someone clapping. "Excellent, excellent," said a malicious voice. "You see, Pylum, I told you the zombies were invincible. They fear nothing and they feel nothing. They are the perfect soldiers, and this test proves it."

The speaker stepped through the doorway. Tash gasped, and even Hoole grunted in surprise. It was Dr. Evazan.

"You're working together!" she cried.

"Naturally," Evazan said. "I use my great scientific genius to animate the corpses while Pylum uses the superstitions of this backward planet to keep the locals away from the cemetery."

"It was the perfect cover," Hoole said. "You used the great supply of bodies here for your experiments. And if anyone did see anything unusual, Pylum simply blamed it on the curse of Necropolis."

"But why?" Tash asked Pylum. "You betrayed all your beliefs."

Pylum rolled his eyes. "You are naive, aren't you? Do you know what it's like to be taunted and mocked by teenagers like Kairn? To be called a madman for upholding the ancient ways? I believed those legends!" Pylum's eyes blazed. "When the jokes became too much to bear, I did the unthinkable. I broke into the Crypt of the Ancients to see the grave of Sycorax itself, to prove that the legends were true! But do you know what I found?" Pylum had worked himself into a rage. He strode over to the stone coffins and heaved one of them open. "This!"

Inside the stone box lay a frail skeleton, wrapped in a tattered gray shroud. The skeleton was so thin, so delicate, that it looked a breath might snap its bones. Pylum almost snarled. "This pile of bones is the mighty Sycorax, the bringer of the curse that has cast a shadow over Necropolis for a thousand years!"

"Pah!" Pylum spat and dropped the stone lid, which crashed back into place with a thunderous boom, sending up a cloud of dust. When the dust cleared, Tash saw that the stone lid had cracked.

Pylum sneered. "Everything I believed in was a lie. There was no curse. I had become the servant of a superstition. When Evazan offered me the chance to make a fortune by helping him, I took it."

"Precisely," Dr. Evazan said. "Everything went according to plan until that bounty hunter showed up, followed by that annoying brat."

"Zak," Tash whispered. "You killed him."

Evazan laughed the most evil laugh she'd ever heard. "Why, no, my dear. *You* killed him. I merely put him in a brief, deathlike coma. You buried him." Evazan checked his wrist chronometer. "In fact if my guess is correct, right now your brother is either running out of air or running out of room to hide from the boneworms."

———

Both were true. In his coffin Zak felt the air become thick and stifling. But that was the least of his concerns.

Above his head he saw the wood of his coffin bulge inward and crack. A fat white wriggling thing appeared, squirming as it tried to enlarge the hole it had made. Using his glowrod Zak poked the worm and it recoiled.

It was a futile gesture. Boneworms were burrowing a dozen holes in his coffin. Confined as he was, Zak couldn't reach them all.

He saw one of the pale, white worms drop into the coffin with him.

Another, then another, followed. Zak felt a sickly wet slap on his cheek, and he felt something crawl right across his mouth. Something else tickled his ear.

"Yaggh!" Zak thought he would be sick. He pulled the boneworms away from his head and flicked them down toward his feet, where the worms splattered against the coffin wall. The boneworms left a trail of slime where they had crawled on his skin. Zak wiped it quickly away, remembering what Evazan had said about the final ingredient to his reanimation serum.

More and more boneworms plopped through the openings in the coffin. He couldn't stop them all. Even if he could, his lungs were burning. He was nearly out of oxygen. He tried to get one more lungful of air as more boneworms wriggled wetly across his skin.

Boom!

Something heavy slammed against the top of his coffin.

Boom!

Again the coffin shivered as though struck by a battering ram.

Boom!

On the third blow, the coffin lid shattered. Someone wrenched away the slivers of wood. Then a gloved hand reached into the coffin, grabbed Zak by the shirt, and hauled him out.

It was Boba Fett.

Zak's head was spinning from lack of oxygen. He saw Boba Fett standing before him, and Deevee standing beside the bounty hunter. He wondered if he was seeing things.

Boba Fett shook him until his head started to clear. Then the bounty hunter rasped, "Where is Evazan?"

Zak tried to speak. "Th-thanks. I thought I was gone for good."

"You would have been, but you have information I need," the bounty hunter stated. "Where is Evazan?"

"Do you know, Zak?" Deevee urged. "Time is short."

Zak took a long breath and felt his lungs fill up at last. That helped his head clear. "Uh, sure. The crypt. Evazan is hiding in the Crypt of the Ancients. Now what . . ."

Boba Fett let him go, and Zak's weakened legs gave out from under him. Deevee helped him back up. "Deevee, how did you know?"

"I found Evazan's files," the droid explained. "And I convinced Boba Fett that you had information he needed. Can you walk?"

"I think so."

"Good. We must hurry."

To Zak's surprise the droid reached down into the coffin. Zak looked down into the hole where he had been buried. The coffin was now full of boneworms wriggling and writhing over one another, searching for the body that had been there—*his* body. He shuddered.

Deevee pulled out a handful of wriggling bone-worms. "We may need these. Let's go."

Tash was too shocked to resist when Evazan's zombie servants dragged her and Uncle Hoole into the hidden chamber, shutting the doors behind them. They were shoved into one of the holding cells, now empty of the zombies that Zak had seen earlier. The door was slammed shut by one of the undead servants. Tash recognized him as Kairn. But she didn't care. She couldn't stop thinking about Zak.

They had buried Zak alive.

She could imagine nothing more horrible.

From behind the bars of the cell, Hoole studied the undead creatures. The scientist in him could not help but be impressed. "Astounding. Complete reanimation." He looked at Evazan. "And you brought yourself back, too, no doubt."

Unable to resist the urge to gloat, Evazan told Hoole the same things he had told Zak.

"The new version of my serum seems to work quite well," he added, giving only a small twitch. "My brain functions and memory are fully intact, as are those of my other test subject." He pointed at Kairn, who guarded the door to the cell. "The serum is now ready for delivery."

"Delivery?" Hoole asked. "To whom?"

Evazan laughed. "Don't insult my intelligence, Doctor Hoole! I may like to gloat over my victims, but do you think I would reveal a secret that important, even to the doomed?" He scratched the blackened scars on the right side of his face. "My employer wouldn't look kindly on that. And I don't intend to be killed a second time."

Even as Evazan spoke, the doors to his secret laboratory exploded inward. Everyone except the zombies ducked for cover as debris flew across the room. Evazan dove behind his examination table. Pylum cowered on the floor with his hands over his ears.

When the smoke cleared, Boba Fett stood framed in the doorway. "Evazan. I do not like to repeat myself."

Evazan snapped, "You won't get the chance. Zombies, destroy him!"

At Evazan's command the undead creatures turned and lumbered toward Boba Fett. Fett moved with the calm efficiency of a trained professional, leveling his blaster and firing with perfect accuracy. Every shot found a mark, blowing the zombies backward a few meters and knocking them to the ground.

But the zombies slowly picked themselves up and started forward again. Fett fired again, blasting more of the zombies out of reach. Again the zombies ignored the gaping wounds in their undead bodies and charged forward.

In the confusion of smoke and noise, Zak and Deevee slipped past Boba Fett and into the chamber. Since Evazan had ordered them to attack the bounty hunter, the zombies ignored Zak and Deevee.

"What are we going to do?" Zak shouted over the noise of Boba Fett's blaster. "Boba Fett can't even stop them."

Deevee raised his vocal volume up a level and said, "I need to get to Evazan's equipment. I think I can reverse the process!" He clutched the handful of bone-worms to his chestplate.

The equipment-covered table was only seven meters away, but Boba Fett's blaster fire turned into a frantic laser storm as he fought to keep the zombies at bay. Stray shots flashed across the room to explode against the far walls, shattering many of Evazan's specimen jars and spilling their slimy contents on the floor. Zak and Deevee had to crawl on their hands and knees to avoid the blaster bolts.

They reached the table, and Deevee immediately dropped the squirming boneworms into a shallow bowl. As they wriggled about, the worms left small slime trails along the glass. Deevee scooped drops of the disgusting liquid out of that bowl and into another, explaining, "Evazan's files explained the reanimation process. I believe I can reverse it by canceling out the chemical substance in the boneworms."

From his hiding place behind the examination table, Evazan yelled to Pylum, who lay crouched nearby. "Pylum, stop them!"

"Stop them yourself!" the Master of Cerements screeched. He bolted for the door and slipped out the same way Zak and Deevee had slipped in.

"Blasted coward," Evazan cursed. He looked around for the nearest zombie. "Kairn! Stop them!" he ordered.

The undead Necropolitan gave a slight twitch and started forward.

Deevee had grabbed hold of several chemicals on Evazan's table and had already begun to mix them together. Zak stood between Kairn and the working droid.

"Kairn, stop! You still have your memory! You're not a zombie slave!"

Kairn twitched. Zak thought he saw a flicker of life in his friend's darkened eyes. "Zak . . ."

"I've almost got it!" Deevee exclaimed.

Kairn growled and took another step forward. "Kairn!" Zak pleaded. "If you've still got your memories then you can still think for yourself. You don't need to follow his orders!"

Kairn blinked. He seemed to be struggling with himself. He took another step forward, then rocked back on his heels. He seemed to be fighting against Evazan's command.

"I have it!" Deevee shouted. He held up a large glass vial of purple liquid. "A small portion of this on the skin will break down the chemical reaction."

"But how do we get it on the zombies?" Zak asked.

Evazan saw his hold on Kairn slipping. "Kairn, get that vial! Bring it to me!"

Kairn lunged forward. He shoved Zak out of the way, then forced the vial out of Deevee's hands.

"Kairn! No!" Zak cried.

The zombie Kairn ignored him. He staggered toward Evazan, who roared in triumph and reached out for the vial.

But Kairn shoved Evazan out of the way as well.

Zak saw Boba Fett firing madly. The bounty hunter seemed to have lost some of his cool calm. His back was to the wall. Every zombie that he blasted away returned again. He probably couldn't hold them off much longer.

Boba Fett fired at the closest zombie, but his shot went wild and the creature lunged at him. Its powerful hands seized his armor and lifted him off his feet. Fett tried to fire his blaster, but before he could, another zombie came up behind the first and splashed a small drop of liquid onto the first creature's face. Instantly the zombie screamed, and its grip weakened. Boba Fett regained his balance as the zombie fell limply to the floor.

Kairn had already done the same to many of the zombies in the crowd. The last of them turned on him, struggling to get the vial from his hands. Kairn fought back, dousing them with the remainder of the liquid. The zombies collapsed. But as the last one fell, it stumbled against Kairn, and some of the purple serum splashed onto him as well. He cried out, then fell forward, collapsing on top of the heap of bodies.

"Blast!" Evazan cursed.

Boba Fett dropped his blaster and pulled the vial out of Kairn's hand. A small pool of purple liquid still lay in the bottom of the glass. Fett hurled it straight at Evazan. The vial shattered as it struck the evil doctor, splashing purple liquid all across his scarred face.

Evazan screeched, dropping to his knees. He gave a violent twitch, then fell face-first to the ground.

Zak and Deevee rushed to the cell and freed Hoole and Tash. Tash threw her arms around her brother, and Zak returned her hug. Unnoticed by either of them, Hoole smiled.

Deevee was the first to speak. "I believe we can make larger quantities of this antidote and spread it around Necropolis. It should take care of the zombies terrorizing the city."

Hoole nodded. "Excellent work, Deevee. It seems you've been able to use your vast brain power after all."

The droid simulated a shrug. "A momentary distraction."

Only Pylum had escaped the violent battle. But he didn't get far. They found his lifeless body at the bottom of the stairs. His neck was broken and his face was frozen in an expression of fear.

"What do you suppose happened to him?" Zak wondered.

Hoole pointed up the stairs to the great iron doors above them. "The doors were too heavy for him to open," Hoole guessed. "He probably slipped while trying to push them and fell down the stairs."

"I would agree with your theory, Master Hoole," Deevee noted, "except that Zak and I were careful to leave the doors open."

"Well, they're closed now," Tash said.

"Then perhaps the Curse of Sycorax found its victim after all," Hoole said darkly.

With Boba Fett's help, they were able to push one of the doors open. As soon as they were out of the crypt, Hoole looked at Boba Fett. "We owe you our thanks."

"You owe nothing," the bounty hunter stated. He stood up. "I like to finish what I start. I wanted Evazan. I needed the boy to lead me to him."

Hoole's next question caught Tash's attention. "And that other matter we discussed earlier?" the Shi'ido asked Boba Fett. "Will you take that job?"

The bounty hunter gave the slightest shake of his head. "Only a fool would take that job."

Then Boba Fett ignited his jetpack and blasted away.

EPILOGUE

Hoole and Deevee worked with the Necropolitans to make more of the antidote. Armed with the serum, they were able to stop the zombies that roamed the city.

Before long all the dead were put to rest and returned to their proper graves. Deevee devised a means to inject the serum into the soil to make sure no bone-worms accidentally revived any bodies yet untouched. The dead would never again rise to trouble Necropolis.

In a new cemetery at the edge of Necropolis, Zak and Tash stood over a single grave. Kairn's name was inscribed on the headstone.

Zak sighed.

"Are you all right?" his sister asked.

"I think so," he replied. "It's just so sad that he was taken away in the first place. Its unfair—just like Mom and Dad." He shook his head. "I've realized something, though. I kept wishing we could have said goodbye to Mom and Dad, but I don't think it would have made the pain go away. And besides, it wasn't really necessary." He put his hand on his heart. "They're never really gone if I keep their memories here."

Some time later Uncle Hoole and Deevee picked them up in their new ship—the *Shroud.*

"Ugh," Tash said. "Are we really taking Evazan's old ship?"

"It was the only ship available in our price range," Hoole replied.

"It's prime!" Zak said, his eyes lighting up for the first time in days.

"Can we at least clean it up and change the name?" Tash asked.

Deevee said, "We can certainly clean it up. But in many cultures, changing a ship's name is bad luck."

"More superstitions," Zak snorted.

"If you dislike superstitions, then you will like this common sense," Hoole said. "I'm considering taking you to the nearest medical facility, Zak."

"What for? I'm fine!"

Hoole frowned. "Perhaps. But we still don't understand everything about Evazan's experiments. You were exposed to his chemicals, and you encountered the boneworms."

Zak shook his head. "Please, Uncle Hoole, the last thing I want after all we've been through is to have doctors poking and prodding me. That serum worked on dead bodies. I mean, do I look like a zombie?"

For a moment Hoole was lost in thought. Then he

said, "Perhaps you are right. But I agree only on the condition that you inform me the moment you experience any illness."

"Deal!" Zak said. "Now, where's the engine room on this thing?"

Zak found a set of tools in the storage bay and then made his way back to the maintenance hatch and popped it open. He smiled happily as he saw the tangled mass of wires and cables. He'd have a great time taking this system apart and putting it back together.

"Me, a zombie?" Zak muttered. "What is he thinking? I haven't felt this good in days."

Zak reached for a hydrospanner, then dropped it as his body gave a sudden, uncontrollable twitch. . . .

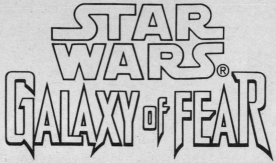

Hoole, Tash, and Zak continue their journeys to the darkest reaches of the galaxy in *Planet Plague,* the next book in the Star Wars: Galaxy of Fear series. *Planet Plague* will be available in stores in April 1997. For a sneak preview of this book, turn the page!

Tash and Deevee both scrambled backward as the blob lunged forward and landed heavily on the spot where they had been standing. The impact caused the creature to flatten out briefly, but then it gathered itself up for another spring. Rolls of squishy brown gel rippled across its surface.

"Deevee, what is it?" Tash cried.

"I'm familiar with more than fifteen billion forms of life in the galaxy," the droid replied with a hint of panic in his electronic voice, "but I've never seen anything like it."

The blob made no sound, except for the disgusting moist slap of its wriggling, fatty skin on the surface of the bridge. Then it sprang again. Tash jumped backward, but this time Deevee was too slow. The oozing creature landed heavily against his legs, sending the droid clattering to the floor of the bridge.

"Help! Help!" Deevee tried to pry himself loose as the blob began to creep up his silver legs.

"Get off him!" Tash yelled.

Tash never knew where the man came from. He seemed to appear out of nowhere. His flight suit was clean but worn, and he wore pilot's gloves that were frayed around the edges. His features were sharp, and his face looked young but very serious. The man wore a blaster at his hip, but he kept it holstered. Without saying a word he kicked the blob with his booted foot. The blob did not react, but the man's boot sank into the wriggling skin up to the ankle. He grunted and pried himself free.

"Use your blaster!" Tash suggested.

"Don't hit me!" Deevee added.

The man ignored them both. He grabbed the upper edge of the blob in his gloved hands and yanked hard. The ooze peeled away from Deevee like a scab. But that only seemed to make the blob angry. It let go of the droid and turned on the rescuer. Two squishy ropes of ooze—almost like arms—suddenly grabbed hold of the man.

"By the Force!" he yelled in surprise as he lost his balance. He staggered backward toward the edge of the high bridge. "I could use some help," he grunted as he tried to lift the blob up over the bridge's guardrail.

Tash hurried to his side, but the man said, "Don't

touch it! Get the droid. And hurry!" The creature's oozing limbs had almost crept up to his shoulders.

Deevee rose stiffly to his feet and shuffled over as fast as his servos would carry him. "I am not programmed to handle this," he muttered as he grabbed hold of the blob. He tried to lift. "By the Maker, this creature is heavier than a human!" Deevee's computer brain automatically transferred more power to his upper servos, and he and the newcomer lifted the blob up and over the guardrail.

"Okay, drop it!" the man ordered, bracing himself against the rail.

Deevee let go, and the blob dropped a few feet. The two thick strands of ooze still clung to the man's shoulders, but as the blob's own weight dragged it down, the ooze ropes stretched thinner and thinner.

"Hold on!" Tash encouraged.

"Good . . . advice!" the man grunted, pulling back against the weight of the suspended blob. Finally the strands of ooze snapped loose. The blob dropped. Tash watched as the creature shrank away beneath them, finally disappearing into the jungle steam. She looked at the man, who was still panting from the effort.

"Thanks!" was all she could manage.

"Yes, indeed!" Deevee added, picking himself up. His legs were covered in slime. "That creature would have turned me into scrap! How fortunate that you happened to be nearby."

"Yeah," the man replied tersely. "Lucky. Did that thing touch either one of you?"

"No. Why? Are they poisonous?" Tash asked.

"Not poisonous." The man cast a nervous glance around.

Not exactly nervous, Tash thought. *More like watchful.*

The man nodded. "I wish I could say the same for my gloves." He held up his hands. The gloves were covered in ooze. He carefully removed them and dropped them over the side of the bridge. Tash watched them flutter toward the ground hundreds of meters below.

Tash pointed to the weapon holstered at the man's hip. "Then why didn't you just blast it?"

At that moment, a hovercar whizzed by. On its side panel, Tash caught a glimpse of the official seal of the Empire. The car zoomed away from them and toward the medical tower.

The man nodded after it. "That's why. Using a blaster might bring a different kind of bug. The *Imperial* kind." As he said this, the man watched Tash closely. She had the feeling that he was trying to judge her reaction to his comment about the Empire.

"What was that blob thing?" she asked, looking over the side. The cries of jungle creatures floated up from below.

The man did not take his eyes off her. "As far as I know, they don't have names. *Blob* is as good a word as any, I guess. They just started creeping out of the jungle a few weeks ago. Before that, no one had seen them. But then these jungles are full of the unexpected."

"And they are allowed to roam at will?" Deevee asked indignantly.

"They seemed pretty harmless before," the man replied. "And they're hard to stop. That sticky ooze allows them to climb up walls and hang from ceilings. Even a fall from this height probably didn't kill that one."

Tash shuddered. She imagined the blob splattering onto the florest floor beneath them, then slowly gathering itself up and making the long climb back up the ziggurat.

Deevee was still in a huff. "Why, then, the local Imperials should do something about them. It's an outrage."

Again the man studied Tash's reaction as he scoffed, "Imperials. What do you expect from them?"

"My name's Tash," she said. "This is DV-9, or Deevee, for short."

The man shook her hand. "I'm Wedge Antilles. Where are you headed?"

Tash shrugged. "We were just going for walk around the city. These pyramids—ziggurats—are pretty impressive."

Wedge nodded. "Listen, how about if I give you a quick walking tour?"

Tash started to reply, "Thanks, but I don't think we—"

"You'll need a guide," Wedge interrupted. "All the bridges between the ziggurats can be confusing. Sometimes I think it would take a Jedi to navigate Mah Dala."

The word was like a magnet that drew Tash's attention straight to Wedge.

"You know about the Jedi?" she asked breathlessly.

The corners of Wedge's mouth turned up in a slight smile. "I've heard of them."

"I've always wanted to be one," Tash said. She turned to Deevee. "I suppose it wouldn't hurt to have a guide."

But the man's manner had triggered Deevee's cautious caretaker programming. "I'm afraid Tash's uncle would not want her to roam a new city with a complete stranger."

Wedge Antilles sighed. "Oh, well. I'm the best guide you'll find around here. I could have shown you some out-of-the-way examples of Gobindi architecture and ancient culture that you'd never find on your own, but if that's how you feel—"

"Culture?" the droid replied with sudden enthusiasm. "Well, I'm sure Master Hoole would not want Tash to miss an educational opportunity. Lead on, Master Antilles."

Wedge led them across the bridge and into the next ziggurat. This one was bustling with activity. The halls inside the flat-topped pyramid were high and wide, with many side corridors and lifts rising up and down. *If all buildings are this well-populated,* Tash told herself, *Mah Dala must be a fairly crowded place.*

The beings came from every corner of the galaxy. Many were human, but there were also large numbers of furry Bothans, Twi'leks with skull tendrils draped across their shoulders, and dozens of other species, walking, crawling, or writhing about. Tash recalled what Hoole had said: The original Gobindi had vanished, and many other species had filled the city they left behind.

They stopped and sat on a bench in the middle of a central plaza as the bustling crowd hurried past.

"This isn't much of a cultural experience," Deevee sniffed. "Crowd-watching is for amateur anthropologists."

Tash ignored him. She was more interested in the man who had saved their lives. "Are you from Gobindi?" Tash asked.

Wedge shook his head. "No. I'm just visiting some friends. I've been here for several weeks, though. Long enough to know the city pretty well. Actually I only planned to stay a few days. But of course with the blockade and all—"

"Blockade?" Tash interrupted. "What blockade?"

Again, the man's eyes seemed to peer inside Tash's head. Tash had the distinct impression that their encounter with Wedge was no accident. It was a strange sensation, but she often had unexplainable feelings about people and events. Lately she'd learned to trust her intuition.

Wedge spoke matter-of-factly. "The blockade of the Gobindi system. According to the Imperial news broadcasts, pirate activity has gotten so bad that the Empire has sent a fleet of Star Destroyers to deal with the problem."

"We saw them," Tash responded. "But we didn't see any pirate ships."

Wedge snorted. "No one's ever seen any pirates. But that doesn't matter to the Empire. They've still ordered all ships to be grounded until they've had time to hunt down the criminals. So everyone's stuck here. No one has come or gone from Gobindi in almost three weeks."

Deevee considered. "You must be mistaken, sir. We just arrived on Gobindi. How is that possible if there is a blockade?"

Wedge raised an eyebrow. "Only Imperials have been allowed to leave or arrive."

So that's what he's after, Tash thought. *He's trying to figure out if we're Imperials!*

"We're *not* Imperials," she replied hotly.

"But your ship was allowed to land—" Wedge replied.

"We're not Imperials!" she repeated.

Wedge held up his hand. "Okay, okay!" Even Tash was surprised at how angry she sounded. She blushed.

She felt foolish, not only for yelling, but for revealing her feelings to this man. She had no idea who he was.

But even so, Tash felt a strong urge that seemed to say *trust him*.

Caught between her two impulses, Tash said nothing. "So, what brings you to Gobindi?" Wedge asked.

"My brother's sick," she replied. "They're examining him at the Infirmary." She pointed to the gray tower rising above the highest ziggurat.

The man's face darkened. He clenched his jaw. "Listen, I'm going to tell you something, even though it might be a mistake. For all I know you could be the daughter of some high-level Imperial officer and you could get me in a lot of trouble. But . . ."

The fear in his voice made Tash's hair stand on end. "What?" she asked.

He nodded toward the Infirmary. "In the past few weeks, no one has come out of there alive."

ABOUT THE AUTHOR

John Whitman has written several interactive adventures for *Where in the World Is Carmen Sandiego?,* as well as many Star Wars stories for audio and print. He is an executive editor for Time Warner AudioBooks and lives in Los Angeles.